DOUGLAS WILSON

Two Williams

DOUGLAS WILSON

Veritas Press, Lancaster, Pennsylvania
©2007 by Veritas Press
(800) 922-5082
www.VeritasPress.com
ISBN 978-1-932168-66-2

The illustrations in this book are pastel drawings that
were made by Judith Hunt (www.huntjudith.com)

Printed in the United States of America.

This book is for
Judah Wilson Merkle and
Seamus James Wilson.
May you always resist
the revolution with courage
and cheerfulness.

Contents

Prologue

This book is the third in a series of stories about the Monroe family in early America. And who knows? If the books keep going we might even work our way down to the present day.

The first book, *Blackthorn Winter,* is about a young man named Thomas Ingle, who lives with his mother Sarah. Thomas's father was lost at sea (probably in a battle with pirates), and Thomas desperately wants to go to sea. His mother finally lets him, reluctantly, and he is apprenticed to a Captain Monroe. In the course of their adventures, Thomas discovers a pirate treasure, Captain Monroe marries Thomas's mother, Sarah, and they buy the land that the treasure is on. The treasure becomes the basis for the Monroe family fortune. The book is set in the very first part of the 1700s, when pirates on the Chesapeake Bay were not uncommon.

The second book in this series is called *Susan Creek* and is set in the late 1740s, the time of the First Great Awakening. The young hero is John Monroe, the grandson of Captain Monroe and Sarah of the first book. His parents are Thomas Monroe and Jane (Thomas had been named after his much older step-brother, Thomas Ingle). John has been apprenticed to sea before he goes back to work in the family business. On this particular voyage to Scotland, he meets a young girl named Jenny Geddes and gets swept up into an adventure involving a British officer who is spying for the French. George Whitefield and his preaching enter the story in several ways, and the story ends with John and Jenny getting married, and with a young son.

This third story concerns the three sons of John and Jenny Monroe and their adventures in the American War for Independence. The oldest son is William, who is an officer in the Continental Navy. We met him as a toddler at the very end of *Susan Creek*. The second son is named Robert, and he is fighting with Morgan's Rifles. They had distinguished themselves at the battle of Saratoga and show up in this book at the battle of Cowpens. But the youngest son, Stephen, is the main character in the book. To find out what happens to *him*, you will just have to read it.

A Tory Tavern

J UST A SHORT WAY OUTSIDE ANNAPOLIS Stephen Monroe had spent the last three weeks sleeping in the stables of his father's country estate. His brother William was due to return from sea to visit the family at any time, and it had been decided that Stephen should finally accompany William back to sea. Until that time, it was very important for him to stay out of sight.

How Stephen came to be living *there* with the draft horses was a small adventure, or joke, depending on how you looked at it, but the consequences were serious enough. Stephen was wanted by the British Redcoat colonel for tying ribbons in the tails of their horses while all the Colonel's staff was taking luncheon at the house of Lady Westmore. The nearby militia was a far greater threat to the Redcoats, but the Colonel was a peacock, and he intended to make an example of Stephen. Besides, it provided an excuse to not take to the field. From the day of that small lark, Stephen had to stay out of sight during the day and spend each night in the stables.

Stephen had been desperate to join the war for liberty for several years, but both his parents had been resistant for reasons that had not been entirely clear to him. His oldest brother William was in the Continental Navy, and the next brother Robert was a lieutenant in the Maryland Line. Why couldn't he go? But the reason Stephen didn't know the reason he couldn't enlist—*that* was the reason. He had been given the reason many times, but for various causes he did not understand them at all. His mother had told him many times that if he understood her, she would be satisfied. But he didn't, and she wasn't. Stephen was something of a hothead, at least for the Monroe clan, and his parents were afraid that he would get a case of liberty fever, worse than he already had it. They were patriots, but they were afraid of some of the patriots they had heard.

But Stephen was hot to fight, and it was a trial to him to obey his parents. However, despite being a hothead, he was obedient, and he tried to be cheerful. Most of the time, he was. When William finally came home, he agreed to take Stephen with him, but he was reluctant for the same reason his parents were. But unfortunately, the zeal of the British colonel was making their choice for them. William and Stephen's mother had talked to William privately about it before he agreed to take Stephen. "He needs to go *somewhere* now," she said. "And we would much prefer it be with someone who cares for him, and who knows our concerns and would honor them."

Late that night, Stephen was summoned in from the stables by a servant, and met in the sitting room with his parents, John and Jenny Monroe, and his brother William. Despite their concerns, which they went over one more time with him, Stephen was hot with excitement. He was going to sea. He was going to see action against the *tyrant.* He did not understand how his parents could be willing to fight for liberty and yet not be excited about liberty in the same way he was. He tried to understand them, but he didn't. They tried to understand him, but they didn't.

At one point near the end of their farewells, he tried to explain a last time. "Just yesterday I was reading Mr. Paine's book *Common Sense . . ."*

William snorted and interrupted. "Mr. Paine is a prodigious fool."

His mother looked with alarm at William, as though to say that she wanted him to restrain Stephen—but not to give him a drubbing. John Monroe looked at the floor, nodding for a moment. Then, looking up, he said, "Perhaps a future conversation will be more fruitful than this one has been.

Stephen, go upstairs for your trunk—it is already packed for you. I want you to take your Bible and leave behind Mr. Paine. That gentleman is all sail and no ballast. When you come back down, we will pray, and you may go."

Three days later, William Monroe sat with his back against the wall of the Jamestown tavern, and next to him sat his young brother Stephen. Stephen was taller than his brother when he was sitting down, and when they were standing he was *almost* taller. But he was also thirteen years the younger, and this meant that although they were not close as brothers, Stephen had always looked up to William as one might an especially important uncle. William had been away at sea for many years—he had left for the first time when Stephen was only three, but he had been faithful to return at regular intervals, and he always kept Stephen's imagination fired with his stories. Of course, it did not take much to keep Stephen's imagination fired, and William always seemed a little stiff and distant. Stephen always wanted to hear more than William was willing to tell.

They had come down to Jamestown from Annapolis because it would be here that Stephen would finally become a midshipman with his brother in the Continental Navy. The two brothers had arrived in Jamestown that afternoon by coach, and when they unfolded themselves from it and stretched in the street, they sought out a place to eat. They were hungry enough that they were not too scrupulous about the tavern they chose and were just now finishing their stew.

William Monroe had been a lieutenant just the previous year, serving under John Paul Jones. He had acquitted himself so well in the battle between the *Serapis* and the *Bon Homme Richard* that when they returned to America, he had been given a commission—a ship of his own, the Susquehanna. It was now the spring of 1780, and it was almost time to sail.

"Tell me again what happened after Captain Jones defied Pearson."

"Well, Pearson called upon our captain to strike his colors, and Captain Jones just stood there, saber in hand, musket balls flying past him, and shouted that he had not yet begun to fight. That stirred every man of us, I don't mind telling you. Their guns had taken out much of our starboard battery, and we didn't have many gunners left either. We sent the marines up into the rigging, and bless them if they didn't shoot like a pack of wizards. They raked the decks of the *Serapis*—I have never seen shooting like that, never."

"What happened next?" Stephen was done with his stew, and his brother was nowhere close. William was not nearly as stiff as he seemed to his brother, and he could tell a sea story as well as any of his mates—but in talking like this to his brother he always felt like he was stoking a fire that was already too hot and high.

"The *Bon Homme Richard* was taking on water, and settling into the sea, sluggish like. We couldn't maneuver, and so Captain Jones tied our bow off to the side of the Serapis, and we just went at it, hammer and tongs. They were preparing a sortie to board us, and so Captain Jones just nodded at me to do something. So I took about seven lads who were with me, and we attacked them, right up the middle. God showed favor to us that day—there was no reason for us to win that battle. And after we won, our ship sank, and we had to sail off in theirs."

"That's *it?* You just told me that there was some fighting, and then it was over."

William laughed in spite of himself. "Well, because of how the ships were lashed together, we had to run single file, and jump from our bowsprit, and not spread out shoulder to shoulder until we were on their forward deck. I was first, and three of us got there before they saw our plan. It was all sabers, and for some moments there all I saw was sabers. A man named Huggins saved my life—twice I think, maybe three times. I had my saber knocked out of my hand by some ruffian, who seemed extremely interested in the color of my insides. Huggins split him like he was chopping wood on a Saturday evening. . . . I got my saber back, and by that time, all seven of us were there. We gave them what for, and that's the truth of it."

Stephen was about to ask yet another question, but he

suddenly yelled, jumping in his seat instead. From across the tavern, a pewter mug sailed right past his head and struck the wall behind him, spattering ale everywhere.

William was on his feet instantly, and Stephen quickly stood up beside him. Stephen had no weapons with him, but William had both a saber and a pistol. From across the tavern, a large figure began to weave toward them. Behind him were several others.

The two brothers waited until their visitor was a few steps away, with only a table between them. "And did ye not know," the man began, "that this is not a Whig establishment? We offer victuals and drink for *Tories,* and for any honest souls who are loyal to their king."

William bent slightly at the waist. "I did not know," he said. "We are strangers in your town. We would be happy, under the present circumstances, to pay our bill, and take our leave." With that he reached toward his pouch to bring out his payment.

The innkeeper (for it was the innkeeper) held up his hand. He stopped for a moment, still weaving, and then lowered his hand again. The men behind him looked slightly apologetic. "Keep your continentals," he said. *"Worthless."*

William started to say that he would pay with silver, but the innkeeper held up his hand again. His dark hair was greasy, tucked behind his right ear. He was in his cups, and when he was in his cups, he was the kind of drunk who wanted to talk politics.

"Here's how ye may pay the bill," he said. "Answer me three questions."

"I see," said Captain Monroe, sucking on his teeth. "And must we answer the questions to your satisfaction? Or just answer the questions?"

"Aye. I take your point." The innkeeper stood there pretending to be puzzled for a moment, and Stephen thought briefly that he was the kind of man that he might like. If he were sober. And if there were no war going.

The innkeeper turned around and looked at the fellows who stood behind him, who had been hanging back somewhat uncertainly. *"You,"* he said, pointing to one of them. "You are the judge. You were a Whig before you got paroled. You've been on both sides. You're the judge. Sit here." With that the innkeeper pulled a chair behind a nearby table and pushed the young man down into it.

"Now," he said, turning around. "King George is my lawful sovereign. Why is he not yours?"

Stephen stepped forward as though he was going to blurt out an answer, but a glance from his brother stopped him. The Monroes had been over this countless times at the dinner table—their father had actually had to *decide* what he was going to do when the war broke out. They had friends and family on both sides, and the issues had not been a simple one for them, except for Stephen.

William rested his hands on his belt, and looked straight into the innkeeper's eyes, which was hard because the innkeeper kept looking at the floor. Captain Monroe was an imposing figure when he was standing, and not eating stew, and when he was this close.

"The king *was* my sovereign. And as such, he had a responsibility as my liege lord to protect me and my family from those who had no such sovereignty, but who sought to exercise it anyway. When Parliament took up the pretence that they were the legislative body for Maryland, when we already had our representatives, the king had a duty to intervene and stay their grasping hand. With Parliament I had nothing to do, and under the ancient rights of Englishmen, I had every right to expect the king to defend us. This duty he refused. And when a liege lord refuses the duty of protection, the vassal is released from the obligations of allegiance."

It was clear to Stephen that the innkeeper had not followed any of this, and it was not surprising to him because *he* had trouble following it. He thought William ought to have simply said that the king was trampling on the rights of man. And had he said this, it would have been on the innkeeper's level, because when *he* usually talked politics, the debate usually amounted to a lusty shout of long life to King George, followed by a fist fight with those who would not drink to his health. Stephen glanced at the young man who had been impressed into the duties of the judge (whose name was Tom) who *was* following the answer, and he was looking increasingly nervous.

The innkeeper cleared his throat when it became obvious that Captain Monroe had finished, and continued, "Does not the good book say that we are to obey the existing authorities?"

Stephen smiled to himself. The good book also had things to say about getting drunk and heaving pewter mugs at the guests. But Captain Monroe just shook his head.

"King Charles claimed that passage as part of his divine right before he lost his head. But the apostle plainly says in that place that the magistrates are God's servants and are not absolute. They are appointed to their servant's station to reward the righteous and punish the evil doer. The apostle does not contemplate the circumstance when the magistrate rewards the evil doer and punishes the righteous. And if my handling of the sacred text be wrong, it is at least the handling of it that was approved by the rulers of England in the Glorious Revolution of 1688. We have maintained nothing in this war for independence except what was established by our rulers as part of common law, before you or I were born."

Stephen looked sideways at Tom again. He was staring at his judge's bench and was drawing pictures with the spilt ale that was there. He seemed absorbed in something else, although he wasn't. Stephen looked up at his brother with exasperation. *Why not just say that friends of tyrants are enemies of God? Why give an answer full of words?*

The innkeeper's face was redder than it had been. He was intent on his fight, but he needed something he could understand. He finally decided to dispense with the finer points of politics. "Have you raised arms against our king?"

"I have. I fought with Captain John Paul Jones when we took the *Serapis . . .*"

With that the innkeeper roared, lowered his head, and ran straight at William. William stepped aside easily and clapped a hand to the innkeeper's back, which sent him sprawling into a cluster of chairs. "Come on, Stephen," William said, and stepped toward the door. They both blinked coming out into the sunlight and were two streets down the way before anyone spoke. William suddenly stopped.

"What is it?"

"We forgot to pay." William was rummaging in his pouch for the coins. "Don't you think he forfeited it? You answered that old loblolly's questions, and to *spare.*"

But William ignored the taunt, turned back, and they made their way back to the inn. When they got there, they found judge Tom leaning against the doorpost, looking up toward the afternoon sun. William touched him on the shoulder, which made him jump, and then offered him the coins. Tom smiled, nodded, and took them.

"You were paroled?" Stephen asked Tom, hoping for a story with some action in it.

"Yes. I fought with the Whig militia when the war broke out. I was captured a year ago in a skirmish near Colcock Creek. I was released on parole and haven't seen action since. My mother is happy about it, fair enough. I sometimes think of breaking my word—especially when I hear things like that in there."

Stephen started to say that every friend of liberty should take the field, but Captain Monroe interrupted, shaking his head. "No—keep your word. We are fighting because the king wouldn't."

With that they began to go, but they stopped when Tom called them back. "One more thing?" William nodded, so he went on. "Don't be hard in your thoughts on my master, old Nob. He lost two boys in the first month of the war. He didn't used to drink. He is a simple man, and I don't think he can make it here if we win. He'll have to go to Halifax."

William nodded, and Stephen didn't know what to do, so they turned toward the harbor. They walked several furlongs when William suddenly said, "Stephen, that's one more thing to remember about my story. Every man we killed on the *Serapis* was a mother's son, and back in some English shire it may be there is a poor innkeeper who drinks too much."

Stephen was silent, but after a moment, he asked—"But

wouldn't you do it again?"

"Of course," William said, "but always remember that war is a splendid and terrible duty. It is not a diversion."

"I will serve you faithfully," he said. Captain Monroe extended his hand, and after the slightest delay Lieutenant Morris took it and left the cabin.

William Monroe turned back to his trunk, now open on his bunk, and took a handful of volumes out. He looked at the spines, silently counting them. There were Blackstone's *Commentary* on the law, Mr. Locke's treatise on toleration, a small quarto volume by Algernon Sidney, a Bible, and Baxter's *Everlasting Rest,* and a handful of others, including a slim and well-marked edition of the *Westminster Confession.*

They cast off the next day and put out to sea—a good breeze behind them and a slight chop to go with it. The *Susquehanna* had good lines and took the waves well. Yankee-built, she was as fine a ship as sailed in the world anywhere, and she sailed with sixteen guns. The entire first day Captain Monroe stood on the afterdeck, enjoying the sea, enjoying his command, enjoying his prospects. The second day he stayed below, helped there by a slow drizzle, going over charts and a few newspapers he had brought with accounts of recent battles in Caroline. The war was prospering there, and he had a free commission to prey on British merchants *en route* to the Caribbean, or to engage any warships he encountered, as he thought prudent. The third day out, they turned south where Captain Monroe thought the slowest merchants could be found—where the lowest fruit might be found hanging, just above the water.

With the exception of the rain on the second day, the weather was perfect their first week at sea. The crew showed themselves a lively group, and the only problem that Captain Monroe noticed was Lieutenant Morris spending more time than he liked with Stephen. The second-in-command customarily took efforts to instruct the midshipmen, and Lieutenant Morris had of course done this, but he would also spend time afterwards visiting with Stephen, leaning on the rail, deep in what appeared to be innocent conversation. And the conversation *was* innocent, although Morris could not be described that way. He had discovered the first day that Stephen had been one of Maryland's liberty boys and that his zeal for the Revolution had something of a different stripe than his brother's. Morris determined by the second day that it would serve him well to plant *some* seeds of dissatisfaction, but nothing too obvious unless Stephen took it up.

At the end of the first week at sea, Captain Monroe had Stephen to his quarters for a private dinner. When they pushed back from the table, William looked at Stephen, arched his eyebrows, and said, "Well, how do you find it? Is it to your liking?"

Stephen looked up eagerly. "Aye," he said. "Although I will like it best when we see action." Like many in his family, Stephen had truly taken to the sea. Not sick at all, he was limber in the rigging, and he knew how to work hard. He had studied diligently while still at home and already knew the rudiments of navigation. In this, he surpassed the other midshipmen, although those two had been on board for six months. Excited, disciplined, and young, he was also pleased with his developing friendship with Lieutenant Morris— although he knew his brother well enough not to say too much about it. Lieutenant Morris had loaned him several other books, one by Mr. Paine, and one by a "hothead reverend" from Massachusetts. At least that is what William Monroe had called him some months ago when his name had come up before in Monroe dinner conversations. But Stephen had read through both of them, and found nothing to object to—unless zeal should be thought objectionable. But he said nothing to his brother about the books.

But he did say something about why it bothered him to have to hide what he was reading. "Brother, back in Annapolis, you called Mr. Paine a prodigious fool. But you fought with John Paul Jones. Our family is solid for liberty. Father is one of the leading patriots in Maryland, and he will almost certainly be in the Continental Congress next session. Our brother fought with Morgan's Rifles at Saratoga. You are a captain in the Continental Navy. I don't understand why you have such distaste for Mr. Paine's fire."

"Because it is a strange fire, and this cause is an altar to God. If it is to remain an altar to God . . ."

At this there was a clatter in the passageway outside, and then a sharp rapping on the door. A tousled head came through the door. "Beg pardon, Cap'n. Ship ahoy, abaft the starboard beam."

The two brothers jumped to their feet and left the cabin, Stephen barely remembering to let his brother go first. Captain Monroe snatched his hat and an eyeglass and took the ladder up without using his hands, Stephen right behind him. A moment later, standing at the starboard rail, Captain Monroe lowered his eyeglass. "Three masts. But what is she? We shall have to snip in and see. Right full rudder! Sound to quarters!"

In spite of himself, Lieutenant Morris watched in admiration. Captain Monroe was making his approach so that if it became apparent that the ship was a British man of war, he could immediately use the wind to cut, turn, and disappear. But the excitement was short-lived, and Stephen was quickly disappointed. The ship was a merchant, separated from her convoy, and as soon as she saw the *Susquehanna,* she turned and tried to lumber away. Low in the water, she was carrying supplies to Lord Cornwallis—clothes, shoes, powder, muskets—supplies that, apart from the red coats, the rebels could put to a much more effective use. But as soon as it became obvious that the *Susquehanna* was much more nimble, the captain of the merchant ship struck his colors. He was a prudent man and not about to go to Davy Jones for the sake of his ungrateful and inanimate cargo. While he was standing at the rail scowling, his irritated thoughts were interrupted by an indignant protest from behind his left shoulder. "Sir, why do you not resist the rebels?"

He bowed his head. "Because, my lady, we have no guns to speak of." The speaker he was answering was Lady Huntington, the daughter of a British brigadier general serving under Cornwallis. Her father, the good general, had summoned her to come and attend him at their headquarters, which was an unusual request but not entirely unusual. There were several other distinguished ladies there already, and Lady Huntington suspected that she was being summoned because her father wanted to marry her off to Major Smythe, a man she admired and detested in equal measure. She detested him almost as much as she did the Americans. This brought her back to the subject of fighting the Americans, and she started to argue with the merchant captain. She thought to herself that she had seen the cargo hold *full* of guns, but when she saw the look on his face, she decided that she would say nothing more, and save her indignation for speaking to the rebels when they boarded.

That boarding was accomplished in short order, and in a brief exchange of words, the merchant captain surrendered his ship to Captain Monroe. "Sir, I relinquish to your rebellious cause most of my worldly cares."

Captain Monroe grinned. "And sir, I accept your kind offer."

Lady Huntington stood back at a distance as haughtily as she knew how, and the effect of her general disapproval was pronounced. At the same time, the first appearance of the

Americans on board unsettled her. At all the fashionable dinners in London that she had attended, where the war was always discussed, Americans were routinely described in such a way as to give her the unquestioned image of the Americans as orangutans, barely able to speak or do business with civilized human beings. But the American captain, standing beside her craven and annoyed merchant captain, provided her with no place in her mind with which to categorize him. She did not know what to say or think, and so she just continued to stand haughtily.

"You were sailing for Charleston?" asked Captain Monroe. The merchantman nodded. "Have your men form a work party to transfer as much of your cargo to us as may be. Start with the munitions. When that is done, you and your first mate come with us." Turning to Lady Huntington, Captain Monroe bowed slightly, and said, "M'lady, it is obvious that you are of some rank and station. When we have arrived back in Jamestown, a message will be sent to the place of your intended destination, and a transfer of your person will be effected. May I have the honor to ask where that may be?"

"With Lord Cornwallis, sir. And I thank you."

He tipped his head slightly and said, "One of the men will bring your belongings over to our ship as well. A lady such as yourself ought not to sail the high seas on a ship without guns."

She flushed and started to reply in a temper but held herself back in time. "I thank you again, sir, for the kindness."

The seamen of the merchant vessel, as soon as it became apparent that they were not going to be slaughtered, turned to the work assigned to them with a will. The holds of the *Susquehanna* rapidly filled, with about a third of the cargo left in the holds of the merchant ship. A prize crew was assigned to the merchant from the *Susquehanna* and instructions given to them to sail for Jamestown in case of separation. When that was done, the last thing left was the transfer of Lady Huntington and her possessions. The sea was calm so the ships had been lashed together, and several rough planks were serving as a gangway between the vessels.

As she stepped onto the deck of the *Susquehanna,* she was met by Captain Monroe again, who took her offered hand and bowed again. "I have made arrangements for you to take my quarters," he said. "It is only for a few days, and I am loathe to subject a lady to any unnecessary hardship."

Her eyebrows went up. "Your manners are most refined, sir." She thought, but did not say, "for an American." She did not say this because that was the kind of thing she knew how to communicate without saying it. But she did say, "One would almost think you had spent time in the salons of Paris."

"I have spent time in the salons of Paris," he said. And he did not say—because he did not need to say it—that the salons of Paris were the native habitat of effete and perfumed sophists. But they *were* well-mannered.

Two sailors escorted her to her new quarters—Captain

Monroe's necessities had already been removed to make room for her.

Stephen was standing with Lieutenant Morris near the after rail, watching all the goods come over. They both watched, without comment, as Lady Huntington came aboard, and the exchanges that followed.

"Your older brother," Lieutenant Morris said, "is a very talented man." The accent of his voice fell slightly on the word *older,* and with a little more emphasis on the word *very.*

"I know that," Stephen said. "But why do you say so?"

"Well, certainly, his gallantry is well known throughout the fleet. Who has not read about it? And the way he approached that merchant just now . . . nothing to call it but smart seamanship. No, he is more than talented—I think the *Susquehanna* has found a great captain."

Stephen flushed with pride, still naïve enough to miss flattery in the mouth of an expert. "Thank you," he said. Lieutenant Morris hesitated, but the hesitation was not visible. "Why, even our Lady Huntington recognized it!" And Lieutenant Morris laughed as though he admired what he detested. "Who could blame him for accepting the homage? I certainly would do the same." Stephen looked across at the Lieutenant Morris, baffled.

At the same moment below decks, Lady Huntington was staring, equally baffled, at Captain Monroe's shelf of books. She reached out and took two of them down, oblivious to the titles. The titles did not matter. He had *books,* out at sea. She could not have been more surprised if she had discovered that Blackbeard the pirate had been an accomplished player of the cello and harpsichord. Impressed and shaken for a brief moment, she then looked more closely at the titles. *Whiggery. Presbyterian rebels. Calvinism.* She put them back and resumed her disdain.

Hot Work

THE WIND WAS CONTRARY, AND THE TWO ships had difficulty making their way back to Jamestown. An expected two or three days turned into four. But late on the third day, the lookout far above the decks of the *Susquehanna* cried out, "Ship ahoy!"

Captain Monroe had been pacing the quarter-deck impatiently, and he swung around immediately, with his eye glass up. One of the first things he saw was the unmistakable colors of the Union Jack.

The prize ship was about a mile ahead, and the British ship just spotted was coming up from astern. Captain Monroe had already given his instructions to the prize crew, and though they saw the man of war also, they just continued on. The only thing they could possibly have done by hanging back would be to make a British victory more lucrative. They could not fight, and so as the looming battle unfolded they disappeared over the horizon.

Captain Monroe immediately began shouting orders, and the *Susquehanna* immediately came about, all her men scrambling to quarters. Stephen, at his station for battle, in spite of all his eagerness to see action, wanted nothing more than for the shooting to start, and yet he felt like some kind of spider was crawling around in the back of his throat. A silence fell over the deck, and for a moment all Stephen could hear was the creak of wood and the recurring slap of water at the bow. No one spoke. Lady Huntington had been taking the air on deck when the sail had been spotted, and Captain Monroe issued a curt order to Stephen.

"Escort the lady to her quarters, instruct her to remain there unless summoned, and return here." Stephen nodded, and approached Lady Huntington courteously. She was not happy about it but nevertheless complied.

When Stephen returned, he heard his brother telling Lieutenant Morris that the English had twenty-four guns, which, he said, "will not be a trouble if we play her right." Lieutenant Morris nodded, appearing to understand what the Captain was going to do. Stephen did not understand at all, but licked his lips as though that would help him watch more closely.

Neither ship made any move that would indicate it

wanted to parley, and no signals were sent. Each was in a posture for battle, and nothing further was necessary. Everyone knew what was happening, and the silence on deck said that a naval battle was the only possibility. The wind was behind the *Susquehanna,* and the British ship was off her port bow, about twenty degrees. Captain Monroe had more of a breeze to work with, and he managed it well. By veering slightly to starboard, Captain Monroe made the English captain think that he was going to wager everything on a broadside, like a fool, even though he was outgunned.

But at the last moment, Captain Monroe shouted, "Left full rudder!" and cut across the bow of the British ship, crossing her like a *T.* This meant that all his eight guns on the starboard side had a smaller target—but at least they could fire at that target, and the British ship could fire at nothing but the empty sea. And Captain Monroe knew from all accounts that his gunners were marksmen—a smaller target was not a problem.

"*Fire!*"

Flame shot out from the starboard side, eight guns recoiling back against the ropes, like lunging tigers. Inside her cabin, Lady Huntington jumped, despite the fact she had thoroughly prepared herself for the inevitable cannon fire. The cannonballs tore lengthways down the deck of the British ship, one of them splintering a portion of the mainmast, and dangerously weakening it. The mast began to lean ominously. In the still aftermath of the volley, across the water, they could hear some violent cursing. The *Susquehanna* spun away, and by the time the English ship came about so that she could return fire, the Americans were nearly out of range. The *Susquehanna* was a smaller ship, lighter and much more maneuverable. Captain Monroe had used all the firepower he had, without allowing the English to punch back at him at all. He could not do this indefinitely, but it was a good way to open the ceremonies.

The *Susquehanna* sailed on ahead of the British ship until there was enough distance to come around again. When that had happened, Captain Monroe gave the order to turn about, and they found themselves in exactly the same position they had been in just about fifteen minutes before. This time the English captain was much more wary and had slowed to about five knots. But Captain Monroe was now ready to trade broadsides. He strode over to the hatch and shouted down to the gunner's mate. "They have four more guns than we do, but here it doesn't signify. They will want to rake us, and if we fire first, and with any luck, enough of their shots will miss to make this an even exchange. Do not rake them. I want all your guns to concentrate on the same spot. Have all guns aim amidships, just above the water line."

"Aye, aye, sir!"

The *Susquehanna* did fire first, and the effect was devastating. A large hole appeared in the side of the English ship, and Stephen watched as one cannon slid out and fell into the sea, followed by two men. But the next moment he realized with a shock that the English still had guns and still intended to use them. The midshipmen were clustered behind Lieutenant Morris, armed with sabers, prepared to lead their sorties when the action got close. When the English broadside came, it raked the *Susquehanna*. All their cannons were filled with scraps of metal, bits of chain, broken glass, and bent nails. Stephen blinked at the roar, and heard the sound of thousands of angry bees whizzing past him, and splintering wood, and cries of pain. Looking to his right, he saw a broken trowel embedded in a nearby mast. He realized that one of the midshipmen who had been standing next to him was gone. Stephen turned around and saw his crumpled form alongside the opposite rail. But their hull was intact, as well as their masts and rigging. The first English volley had apparently consisted mostly of grapeshot and hard scraps, and about ten Americans were down.

The *Susquehanna's* gunner's mate had his cannons reloaded before they had completed their passage of the enemy ship, and he was ready to fire a second broadside. Captain Monroe was leaning over the hatch, roaring below.

"Do the same again. Widen the hole! *Fire!*"

Stephen watched with wide eyes as the second round slammed into the side of the enemy. Water plumed and wood splintered. He turned away for a moment and looked down the length of the *Susquehanna*. His eyes got wide again when he saw Lady Huntington, standing on the ladder of the forward hatch, looking out at the battle. The hatch surrounded her like a picture frame, and her white dress stood out sharply against the blackness behind her. He was about to run over and scold her back down below when a shout from his older brother interrupted him.

"Prepare to board!"

The British ship was listing dangerously to port. She did not appear to be in immediate danger of sinking, but she had taken on enough water to remove a great deal of the maneuverability she had—and she was the heavier ship to begin with. She was also listing enough that it was difficult to elevate her guns high enough to reach the *Susquehanna*. One volley was enough to tell Captain Monroe how limited their range now was. The *Susquehanna* furled her sails, and was standing off, just out of range of the British guns that by now could only fire about twenty yards.

Captain Monroe walked over the hatch again and said, "This time, aim just aft of the hole we have already made. Concentration!"

"Aye, aye, sir!"

"*Fire!*"

Captain Monroe's tactics were strikingly effective, but a fortunate providence was also favoring them. Their cannon-balls tore an awful hole that was now about fifteen yards wide.

Immediately after the volley, Captain Monroe leapt up on the rail, holding the rigging with his left hand, saber in his right. "Will you strike your colors?" No reply came, except for a single musket shot from a British marine that tore Captain Monroe's hat off. A lusty cheer arose among the English, and Stephen smiled in spite of himself. He looked back to where Lady Huntington was, and she was still there, looking out at the carnage with a fascinated mixture of admiration and horror. He also noticed that she was watching his brother ... in just the same way. He had no time now to send her back below, and besides, the English cannon were not a threat anymore.

In a moment of eerie silence, across the water, they heard the cry, "Prepare to repel boarders!" The enemy ship could not return fire with cannon and the two ships drifted closer together. Captain Monroe said something to Lieutenant Morris, who then shouted orders to some of the crew. About five men appeared, standing with grappling hooks at the ready.

"One more volley of cannon, and then the hooks!"

"Aye, aye!"

"This time, rake her decks!"

A faint *aye aye* came up from below decks. The gunner's mate had anticipated this order, and his men were ready with their barrels of grapeshot, broken glass, and nails.

"Fire!"

The British crew was still reeling from the savage volley when the hooks started to fall on her decks, catching at her rails, and the Americans began to haul on the lines. The ships began to close. Stephen lined up with his men, a party of about ten seamen, all armed with sabers and pistols. Gunsmoke floated past them, momentarily obscuring their view of the enemy ship. Behind them, Stephen could hear the groans of some of the wounded. There were three other columns of men, all prepared to board in the same way. One was led by Lieutenant Morris, one by another midshipman, and one by one of the mates.

The two ships slammed together, and the boarding parties poured over the rail. The fact that the English ship was listing so far to port meant that the Americans could jump down from above. Stephen was the first to board, and he struck down the first two men he encountered. He turned to face a third and felt something that was like a sudden stinging lash on his left cheek. Stephen staggered backward and fell to the deck. He struggled back to his knees and felt his cheek, which was bleeding profusely. The man he had been about to face was down, laid out by Captain Monroe, who had seen all the parties board and then followed up where he thought the hottest work would be. Stephen felt his cheek, and under the blood he could feel a long splinter of wood hanging down. He could still see out of his left eye.

He got to his feet heavily, and took two steps back toward the action. He could see Lieutenant Morris fighting furiously with two sailors and behind him a marine lunging toward him with a bayoneted musket. Stephen tried to shout a warning, but the marine suddenly fell when Captain Monroe stepped up and took off his head. The two men that Lieutenant Morris was fighting saw what had happened, and their sails suddenly went slack. They threw their swords on the deck, and other men around them began to do the same. Lieutenant Morris turned around to look at Captain Monroe, and instead of gratitude, Stephen was shocked to hear Lieutenant Morris shouting, "You cannot give quarter now!"

Captain Monroe ignored him. "Throw down your weapons!" More and more English sailors were doing so. The captain turned around to issue his command for surrender in the opposite direction. Lieutenant Morris stepped in front of him, his face flushed and angry. "You cannot give quarter!"

"But I do."

"Liberty is not won by the soft-hearted! If our liberty requires blood, then our liberty calls for men who are willing to *shed* it."

"Mr. Morris, please stand aside." Captain Monroe stared at him coldly, and after a long moment, Lieutenant Morris bowed stiffly at the waist, and stepped aside.

Toward the bow, some fighting was still going on, although more and more of the English were asking for quarter. Stephen took another step forward when a stray

musket ball caught him in the left shoulder, spun him around, and dropped him to the deck.

When he opened his eyes again, he was completely confused. Everything was silent. He lifted his head, barely, and saw that he was back on the *Susquehanna,* on the afterdeck. He was the last in a row of wounded men. Next to him, he could see Lady Huntington stooped over a patient, tying a bandage off. Stephen noted absently that the man she was treating was wearing the clothes of a British sailor. Briskly finishing, she turned to Stephen and smiled when she saw he was awake.

As she began to pull back his shirt, Captain Monroe walked up behind her. "Madam, I greatly thank you for agreeing to help our surgeon. This is my brother, and so I ask you give him particular consideration."

Lady Huntington stopped for a moment, astonished.

"He is your brother? And you did not have him treated first?"

Captain Monroe shook his head. "No. Had his life been in danger. But other men needed attention first."

"May I take it that we won?" Stephen croaked.

"*You* won," Lady Huntington said.

Captain Monroe smiled, a little grimly. "Yes, we won. But the *H.M.S. Splendor* sank, leaving us with fifty prisoners, with only ten men to guard them. I'll have to ask you to recover a little more quickly than perhaps you would otherwise do."

Stephen tried to move his left arm and was barely successful. "I don't think this is that bad."

"I will decide that," said Lady Huntington.

Stephen suddenly remembered his face, and reached up to touch it gingerly. All he could feel was crusted blood. "I must look a sight," he said.

"That you certainly do," his brother said. "And it may leave a garish scar to distress your mother and impress all the maidens around Annapolis. But you have long needed something to offset the perfection of your features."

Stephen grinned and leaned back, satisfied. He had been through his first battle, and he had not disgraced himself, or his family. He was alive, and though both wounds were throbbing, he could tell that he would be alright.

"We won," he said. "And may I please have a drink of water?"

Lady Huntington turned around and beckoned someone, and a man quickly came up with a wooden bucket of water and a sponge. He knelt down beside Stephen's head, lifted it up, and swabbed around his mouth with the sponge. He then squeezed the cold water into Stephen's mouth. Stephen thought it was the most delicious moment of his life.

Lady Huntington was looking at his shoulder wound, trying to decide how to dress it. The surgeon was working on those wounds where bones had to be set or musket balls needed to be dug out. Lady Huntington had been given the task of cleaning and dressing those wounds that would require little else, and it soon appeared that Stephen was in that category.

"Does my brother know that you disobeyed to watch the battle?" Stephen asked.

Lady Huntington smiled. "Not that he has mentioned. And I see no need to mention it to him. He is not my captain."

"Well, he is mine," said Stephen. "But all is well."

Lady Huntington, for all her refined upbringing, was very capable at what she was doing. She dressed Stephen's shoulder wound in short order and told him he would be up and about in a trice, and then she turned to tend the wound on his cheek. As she was wiping away the blood, she asked, "And how old is your brother?"

Stephen blinked, surprised. A witticism occurred to him, but he thought better of it. "Thirteen years older than I am," he said.

"Is this his first command?" she asked.

"First command, and first engagement," Stephen replied. "God has answered our prayers for victory. I prayed mightily for this, I have to say."

"I see," she said. "And do you think God takes sides in affairs such as this? Suppose I prayed mightily that you would *not* win? How would God decide?"

Stephen had never thought of that. He knew there were Christian people on both sides of the Atlantic, and they would all presumably be praying for their own men and boys, off at war. He was silent, but because he was wounded, he thought he could get away with not answering. His first thought was to ask his brother. His second was to ask Lieutenant Morris. And he realized that he would almost certainly get completely different answers from them.

Tired Nations of Christendom

 T WAS A WEEK LATER,
and the *Susquehanna* had been tied up in Jamestown
for almost the entire time. A crew had spent the first several
days repairing damage to the ship, which was slight. The
prize merchant had made it safely back to port before them,
and Captain Monroe was now the toast of the town.
Messengers had ridden off excitedly to the north to have
reports of this victory at sea published in newspapers.

Several plantation owners in the area who were Whigs held
a ball to celebrate the victory and were excited enough about it
to invite the governor, who had decided to come. Captain
Monroe, Lieutenant Morris, and two other officers from
adjoining ships attended the ball, and there was no little

confusion and discussion beforehand about what to do with Lady Huntington. Finally, Captain Monroe approached her to invite her to attend, and did so with obvious discomposure.

"I do not want to insult a lady, and I confess that my manners are not equal to this occasion. To neglect to offer an invitation to a lady of your stature would, as it seems to me, be a breech of manners to be spoken of for years. At the same time, to invite you to a ball where you will be surrounded by Whigs and rebels would also offer insult to your sensibilities. I defer to your sentiments; as to mine, they do not signify."

Lady Huntington smiled, a little grimly he thought, and nodded her head that she would come. As he thanked her and turned to go, she thanked him as well, and said she understood the position he was in. But the day after they returned from the ball, Lady Huntington was silent, Captain Monroe was morose, and Lieutenant Morris appeared to be quietly furious. Stephen was very curious, and he made some faces, but could get no one to say anything.

Stephen had spent three days in bed, during the last of which he was entirely miserable, wanting desperately to get up. Finally he had gotten permission from Lady Huntington and the surgeon, and though he was weak and sore, he felt well enough to remain out of his bunk for the entire day. By the end of the week, he felt well enough to return to his work, which he was eager to do.

On Sunday, he attended divine services with his brother

in town, where the parson was markedly uninspired. On the way back to the ship, Captain Monroe snorted, "I never heard such learned murmuring in my life."

The next day Stephen was assigned to be in the party that escorted Lady Huntington to the camp of Lord Cornwallis under a flag of truce. Lieutenant Morris was given charge of the party, which consisted of Stephen and two sailors picked out by Lieutenant Morris.

The British army was a long way south, and the party expected the round trip to take several weeks. A carriage and horse was borrowed from a sympathetic Whig landowner, and they finally set out mid-morning. Lady Huntington sat by herself in the carriage, one of the sailors drove, one rode on ahead, while Stephen and Lieutenant Morris rode behind, quietly talking. Lady Huntington could occasionally hear wisps of the conversation, not enough to understand what they were talking about, but enough to make her worry for Stephen. All the men were armed as though they were prepared to scale the walls of a fort filled with courageous men.

They treated her courteously and well, Stephen particularly. They only had to stay in one inn along the way; the other evenings they were lodged by hospitable Whig planters. When they were two days away from Cornwallis, in his conversations with Stephen, Lieutenant Morris raised the questions of the new world after the war. As far as Stephen was concerned, they were simply talking politics, which he had always loved to do.

But for Lieutenant Morris the issues ran far deeper. He was a man with no religion, and the cause of liberty had fully taken that place. Stephen was simply young and loved the excitement of all fervency and zeal. He enjoyed reading Mr. Paine because it made his blood hot, while Lieutenant Morris enjoyed reading Mr. Paine because he understood him.

"After the war . . . if we win it," Lieutenant Morris said, "we will have the opportunity to throw off the shackles of centuries. The war started over just a few of those shackles, but even our representatives in Congress have always intended to keep most of them firmly in place. And that will happen unless the heat of the war rises to prevent them from establishing just another nation like all the others we have left behind."

"My brother says that is what he wants—to return to the ancient rights of Englishmen. He says he is not fighting for a new order—the rule of Parliament over the colonies is the new order, far too new for him. He wants to throw that off and go back."

"Aye. And I believe him. But laddie . . ." Lieutenant Morris stopped.

Stephen looked at him curiously. "Go on," he said.

"I have no desire to speak ill of your brother. He is a very great man, a master seaman. The way he won that battle the other day was a wondrous sight. I have nothing but admiration for his abilities. But . . ."

"But . . ." Stephen waited.

"But by showing quarter to those prisoners, he threw the fruit of that victory away. He does not know the nature of the war we are in. He thinks it a battle between two tired nations of Christendom, after which everything returns to normal. But that 'normal' means the suffocating weight of centuries of tradition, the mumbled superstitions of these damned clergymen—I even heard your brother note one such clergyman the other day—the shackles that we now have the opportunity to strike off. But it will not happen unless we see the need to fight as though a new world is being born— because it is. And that means we must make the sacrifice of throwing away the false sentiment of . . . of chivalry. This is a hard mercy, and only a few men see it now. But future generations will see the fruit of it."

Throughout the day, Stephen continued to argue half-heartedly with Lieutenant Morris, wondering why he used the word *shackles* so much. He was affected by it more than he knew. Lieutenant Morris continued. "Your brother and I are both warriors, and he is a great one. I touch my cap to him. But we are warriors of differing traditions. I believe that his tradition is coming to an ignominious close—the irony is that we are fighting that tradition in its British form, and many of those on our side represent exactly what we really ought to be fighting against everywhere. Those Presbyterian parsons up north, for example."

"My family is Presbyterian," Stephen remarked mildly,

but for some reason he did not say that he was.

"And they are great fighters. For sheer cussedness, there is no one better. But we also need great thinkers—men like Mr. Paine who see that the new order of the ages really is coming."

Stephen was not at all sure how to answer the questions that Lieutenant Morris was bringing up, and he was silent for a time. After a few moments, he thought to bring up the question Lady Huntington had raised the week before. "What would you say to this?" Stephen asked. "Before our battle with the *Splendor*, I prayed that we would win. But Lady Huntington asked me what I would say if she told me that she had prayed that we would lose. I am not sure she did pray. But she could have."

At this, Lieutenant Morris laughed out loud. Stephen had known that he was a freethinker, rejecting all religion, but he was still shocked to hear it so openly expressed. "That is precisely the question that caused me to open my eyes wide as a small boy. In the course of a few days, I heard two pious gentlemen who went to our church express great confidence that God would answer their prayers. One was a merchant who wanted fair weather so his ships could put out to sea. The other was a farmer who was confident that God would send foul weather so that his crops would get their needed rain. I thought about it for ten minutes and settled *my* mind on the subject. But I had to wait until I was grown to say what I thought."

Stephen grew silent. He knew his brother, *and* his father,

would answer the question quite differently, but he was not sure how. The simplicity of Lieutenant Morris's approach was unsettling. But the intensity behind it was unsettling in another way. Stephen changed the subject.

Two days later, they were within a few miles of the British encampment. Stephen was given the flag of truce and rode out ahead of their party to encounter the first English pickets that were bound to be stationed along the road. Stephen came on two pickets within a mile or so, and when the message was delivered, one of them went galloping off to the camp to receive instructions. The remaining guard was not talkative at all and simply motioned for Stephen to graze his horse under a spreading elm tree on the opposite side of the road from him. This Stephen was happy to do and sat with his back against the tree watching his horse for an hour or more. He wondered vaguely what was taking so long but was happy for the rest.

When two hours had passed, he heard the clop of hooves along the road and stood up, realizing he had fallen asleep. Looking down the road, he saw a group of three coming toward them—the original messenger and two officers. Both officers were in Redcoats, but one of them had a blue plume on his helmet that rose straight up. He sat in the saddle like a straight poker, and had a regal and imperious air about him. Stephen looked down at himself and all of a sudden felt grubby and unkempt.

The party rode up, and Stephen walked out into the road,

holding the reins of his horse, his flag in his left hand. "Are you the rebel messenger?" the imperious one asked.

"I am," said Stephen.

"And so your forces have no gentlemen to escort the Lady Huntington?"

Stephen flushed with anger and embarrassment, and swallowed several retorts that occurred to him. "Will you grant us passage?"

The officer sat still on his horse for a moment. Then Major Smythe—for that was his name—nodded curtly.

Stephen mounted his horse easily, and touched his tri-corner hat. "Our assignment is to bring the lady all the way to your camp. But we should do that regardless, for she is riding in a carriage that we must return."

Major Smythe nodded again, contemptuously, and Stephen wheeled his horse to go. All the way back to their small party, he seethed quietly. As he rode up to them, Lieutenant Morris rode out to meet him. "Have they given safe passage?"

"Aye. In as churlish a manner as I have ever seen."

Lieutenant Morris chuckled bitterly. "Let us ride into the bastion of civilization then."

Within about twenty minutes, they began to approach the waiting British contingent. When they were just a few yards away, Major Smythe rode up to Lady Huntington's carriage, ignoring Lieutenant Morris completely. Leaning slightly on his horse, he touched his helmet with impeccable manners.

"Lady Huntington, are you well?"

"I am quite well," she replied.

"Have these ruffians kept their distance?"

"They have. But . . ."

This was too much for Lieutenant Morris, who suddenly intruded himself into the conversation. "The Lady Huntington is being returned to your forces as a courtesy from Captain Monroe of the *Susquehanna.* With your permission, we will accompany her to your camp to ensure her safety."

In reply, Major Smythe just stared, and Lieutenant Morris stared back. Even when they all turned their horses toward the camp, the tension remained in the air, and Lieutenant Morris looked like he would start fighting if someone gave him a shilling for the trouble. He was already an angry man, and Major Smythe represented everything he thought detestable about the world. And whatever Stephen thought about their previous conversation, he agreed with *that.* They all rode in silence, and when they came into the English camp, Stephen saw that nothing about the size of their forces was really visible from the road they were on—which explained why they had not been blindfolded. They all rode in silence up to a commandeered white plantation house. The drive up to the house was fenced on both sides with a row of enormous trees, and Spanish moss hanging down made the approach almost into a romantic adventure.

Standing on the front porch was Lord Cornwallis and Lady Huntington's father, the Lord Huntington, and a few other assorted officers. When the carriage rolled to a stop, Lady Huntington waited quite properly for Major Smythe to dismount and offer her his hand. When he did so, he then escorted her toward the house. She curtsied, quite formally, both to Lord Cornwallis and her father, which Stephen thought was odd.

At the top of the stair, Major Smythe turned and gave a command to his soldiers. "Escort the rabble back," he said.

"Thank you, *gentlemen*," Lady Huntington said pointedly. Stephen smiled, and they all wheeled their horses and trotted down the drive.

Lieutenant Morris fumed for miles, and Stephen was quiet and thoughtful. One of the sailors tied his horse to the back of the carriage, and sat behind his mate in the shade of the carriage, pretending to be a great lady. They rode slowly into mid-afternoon, and Stephen grew, as he put it to himself, a "powerful thirst." A distant noise up the road made Stephen look up and squint against the sunlight, and he saw a man galloping down towards them. He pulled up violently when he came within earshot, and his horse cantered in place, foaming from a very hard ride.

"No king . . ."

"But Jesus," Stephen answered. "No king but Jesus." Lieutenant Morris grimaced, but at least they now knew this fellow was not riding for King George.

"I am a scout for Captain Dunstan of the militia, coming up to this road behind you, several miles back. The Tory militia is on the move and has taken Carston just up the road ahead. They are astraddle the highway now, as pleased with themselves as can be. If you are heading back to Jamestown, you'll need to take another way."

Lieutenant Morris swore in disgust and sat on his horse scratching the back of his head. After a moment, he told the scout who they were and what they had been doing. "Can we go back and join up with you all for a night, and then head north to go around?"

The scout nodded cheerfully. "Captain Dunstan takes all comers. Come with me."

With that, they turned around and began to move back down the road.

"Captain Dunstan?"

"Oh, everybody knows Captain Dunstan," the scout said, "but I forget you are navy boys. We just came up from the south, burning out Tory farms and gathering supplies for the main army. General Gates didn't order us to do that, but at the same time, he don't ask too many questions. And he likes getting the food."

"Burning out Tory farms?" Stephen started to speak, but then thought better of it. About an hour later, they rode up to a make-shift camp that had not been there when they passed through earlier in the day. The scout escorted them to the tent at the center of the camp, introduced them to the captain, gave his report, and left them. The captain was a grim, smoke-dried man and accepted their account of themselves at face value. Lieutenant Morris was invited to the officer's mess, and the others were shown the way to a tent on the edge of the camp and to the pot hanging over the central fire in the camp.

As they were leaving, Lieutenant Morris turned and said to them, "Be ready to set out first thing in the morning. If we have to detour around the Tory camp, that'll be several extra days . . ."

But Captain Dunstan interrupted. "No need to do that. We intend to head up the road in the morning and poke a hole in their militia. You look like you can fight, even if you're not on a rolling deck. Come with us, join in the action, and then be on your way when we are done chasing them into the woods."

Lieutenant Morris looked at him, and then at Stephen. Stephen nodded, eager to accept. Lieutenant Morris looked back at the captain and agreed. As Stephen and the sailors went off, Stephen laughed out loud and said to the sailors, "We will have to figure out what to do with this carriage though. And you will have to stop being quite so genteel a lady."

The Hinge that Turned

STEPHEN SAT ON THE BACK OF HIS HORSE and tried to make out the figures moving silently around him in the early morning. When it came to preparing for action, Captain Dunstan's forces were obviously well-disciplined, although from the stories told last night, they did not appear to be too scrupulous when it came to some of the Ten Commandments.

Several horses had been found for the two sailors, and the carriage was hitched up and drawn along behind them. They had decided that they would just bring the carriage along, and tie the horses off just before they made their final approach. They could just come back for the carriage after the battle. Stephen laughed at the sailors next to him. "You look just like two sacks of meal stealing the miller's horses."

One just sat sullenly, still half asleep, while the other snorted. "Give me a rolling deck, and I'll show you what a sack of meal can do."

After about fifteen minutes Stephen heard an order given in the distance, and a column began to form on the road. When they set off briskly, Stephen heard a soldier up ahead say, "We should be there by sunrise." They were about halfway back in the column, but as the light grew, they could start to make out what was happening at the head whenever the road curved. And just before sunrise, Stephen saw two scouts galloping frantically back toward the head of the column. Captain Dunstan held up his hand, signaling a stop, and even though no one could possibly hear, everyone in the column was absolutely quiet, acting as though they *could* hear. Captain Dunstan leaned forward on his horse, and the two scouts were both gesturing and talking at the same time. Captain Dunstan suddenly sat straight up again and turned to signal his troops again. The troop had been two abreast, but now the columns just ahead of Stephen veered to the right and left and smoothly advanced alongside the front of the column, so that they were four abreast—and Stephen was right near the head of the force on the right side. He looked over and saw Lieutenant Morris, looking extremely grim, on the left. Captain Dunstan sat motionless, and when he was satisfied that everyone was in place, he turned again and set his horse at a canter.

They went this way for about half a mile, and then when they came to the final bend in the road they broke into a gallop. The Tory militia had camped on this side of Carston, and had been lazy about setting out enough pickets. There were only two on the road, and there was nothing for them to do but bolt into the thicket on the side of the road. The rebels galloped past them, and Stephen could see the encampment up ahead, smoke from the campfires curling up into the morning air. There was no sound but the pounding of the hooves on the dirt road, and then suddenly, there was a brief abortive blast from a panicked bugler in the camp. The surprise was almost total. Men were tumbling out of their tents, looking around frantically for their weapons, and there were not enough men ready to form any line of resistance. When the column of horses hit the encampment, the rout was complete, and Tories were scattering everywhere. On the far side of the camp, the rebel horses wheeled and individual horsemen began pursuing almost at whim. There was very little fighting. *Heels and elbows!* Stephen thought.

Within a few moments, Stephen had teamed up with Lieutenant Morris and the sailors again. "I'm glad we got an early start," Stephen grinned. Lieutenant Morris nodded curtly, and Stephen wondered if he was upset because there had not been more action. After about a half hour of hunting down scattered Tories, along with some false alarms, Stephen thought they were done. "I'll go back and get the carriage," he volunteered. Lieutenant Morris arranged to go slowly, and they would wait for him just up the road on the far side of Carstan.

Stephen spurred his horse and trotted happily back to where the carriage was. When he got there, he discovered that the horses had not been tied securely and had wandered off. He was half an hour looking for them, and when he was back on the road he was a little flustered and blown. And leading the carriage without a driver proved to be a little more awkward than he thought it would be. And what with one thing and another, Stephen was about an hour later than he thought he should have been when he came out the other side of the town.

There was a river about a mile past Carston, and the river was at the bottom of a deep ravine—and the road was a torturous set of switchbacks down to the ford, where they were supposed to meet up. When Stephen came to the crest of the ravine, he could look down and see little bits of the road here and there, all the way down to the bottom. As he started down, he saw his companions waiting for him there but then took a sudden, second glance. Three figures were advancing out of the woods, hands held high. *Oh, no,* Stephen thought. *Prisoners will sure slow us down.* And he spurred his horse down to the right.

With the carriage tangling him up at every turn, it took him about fifteen minutes to get to the bottom. When he came around the last bend before the ford, he was turned around in the saddle, trying to keep the carriage straight. And when he turned back around to the front, his face went white, and he could not speak for a moment.

"What are you *doing?*" he finally cried.

Lieutenant Morris turned around calmly, as if he had been interrupted in the middle a quiet conversation. "Why, Stephen, we have been expecting you," he said. "We are hanging us some Tories."

There was a tall oak next to the stream with a branch extending back toward the road. Three ropes had been thrown over the branch, and three young men were standing on the ground under the branch with nooses around their necks, hands tied behind their backs. Their shirts were pulled over their heads, but Stephen could tell they were all young men. Two of them were apparently negro servants, and one of the servants was sobbing and muttering under his breath. The other two just stood quietly.

"I am glad you got here in time," Lieutenant Morris said.

Stephen rode up to them slowly, while trying to think. "You can't do this," he finally said.

"Remember our conversation, Stephen," Lieutenant Morris said. "These things are not topics for philosophers to discuss over a game of whist. They have immediate and pressing applications. And what this country needs is fewer Tories."

"But they . . ." Stephen started, and then stopped. He had

been going to say, "But they surrendered," when he realized that this would reveal that he had seen them from the ridge. And he did not know what he was going to do yet. And saying *that* would make him decide.

"But what?" Lieutenant Morris asked.

"I don't mind fighting Redcoats. And I don't mind killing Tories. I know we need to do that. But this seems like *murder.*"

"I know it seems that way—if you listen to your superstitions. You would happily have killed any of these bucks two hours ago, and not now? This is a new world being born, Stephen, and we must soon enough be going."

Stephen knew now that if he mentioned that he had seen the prisoners asking for quarter it would make no difference. He felt as though he had been suddenly thrown off a cliff, and he was flailing around for something to catch onto. He knew that he was going to have to choose between Lieutenant Morris's revolution and his brother's. And his father's. He came to understand years later why he chose the way he did, but at the moment he did not know anything in the world.

He looked at the sailors, standing by the head of the horse that had the first rope tied to it. "Do you agree with the lieutenant?" he asked.

"What does it look like, laddie?"

Stephen was alongside them all now, and thought he was in a position to decide. And so he decided. He had two loaded pistols in this belt, ready for the fight at Carstan that had never happened, and a saber at his left side. With one motion he drew the saber with his right hand and pistol with his left. "Step away from the horses," he said.

Instead of obeying, all three men lurched for their weapons, and Stephen calmly shot one of the sailors through the neck. He fell to the ground gasping and within seconds was still. Stephen spurred his horse toward Lieutenant Morris who was at his saddle, trying to get his saber loose, and he slashed at him, striking him on the left shoulder. Lieutenant Morris fell and then staggered to his feet. Stephen pulled his second pistol, turned quickly to see where the other sailor was, and shot him in the chest. Spinning around again, he saw that Lieutenant Morris had made it to the carriage, and was turning it around to flee up the hill. Torn for a moment between pursuit and untying the prisoners, Stephen decided to stay with the prisoners. He knew that he either had to kill Lieutenant Morris or get back to the *Susquehanna* first. He was at the ford, which meant that he should have no problem getting back to his brother with the story first.

He turned to the prisoners, who were standing motionless, afraid to move in any direction. He started with the closest one, the servant who had been sobbing, and taking his knife from his belt, he cut the noose away from his neck. He pulled the shirt down off his face, and was confronted with an odd mixture of waxing gratitude and waning terror.

"*Thank* you," he said. The second servant was much calmer and just looked at him and nodded gratefully.

When he performed the same service for the young white man, he cut the noose away, pulled the shirt down, and then stepped back in astonishment. "George!" he said. "Cousin!" The young man blinked in surprise, started to speak, and then said nothing.

Stephen had stepped back several paces. "Are you George Ingle?" he asked at last, his voice quavering.

"I am your cousin," George replied haughtily. He had been badly frightened at the prospect of being hanged, and anger over Lieutenant Morris's treatment of them was now flooding in to replace the departing fear.

Stephen stooped down and sat on his heels, feeling sick to his stomach. He had just killed two men, and wounded a third, but the fact that he had almost acquiesced in the hanging of his cousin was what made him ill. After a moment, he got up and walked over to a nearby bush and was sick. When he had recovered himself, he walked back over to the three men who just stood, watching him.

"Will you sign a parole?" Stephen asked.

"Do you expect me to thank you for killing your murderous companions?"

Stephen shook his head. "You may do as you please in that regard."

"I will sign a parole."

With that, Stephen stepped around behind them, taking out his knife again. The ropes were tight, and Stephen had some difficulty getting through them without cutting their hands. And with his cousin, unhappily, he *did* cut him on the right hand. When Stephen was done, he got a piece of paper and a quill pen out of his pack, and brought it to George, who scribbled angrily for a moment and then handed it to him.

"You may feel I am lacking in courtesy for not thanking you. But I do not thank you. Your companions, with whom you were clearly in arms together, promised us quarter and then undertook to commit foul and treacherous murder. You are not as advanced in their knavery, that is clear enough, but you are in the same wretched cause. If you were to come with us, I could bring myself to thank you." His conscience was bothering him, his pride was injured, and he was still badly frightened. He was only about five years older than Stephen. The last time they had been together, about ten years earlier, they had spent a delightful afternoon playing in the tobacco fields together.

"I can't take these horses with me. You may have them." With that, Stephen turned and pulled the two dead sailors off the road, buried them in leaves, stood over them quietly for a moment, trying to remember the right words from the funeral prayers he had heard as a boy. The three freed men were getting their horses ready, and when Stephen came back and mounted, they were also ready to go. Stephen touched his hat, and his cousin just looked back at him stonily. The two servants behind George both mouthed *thank you* silently.

When Stephen was on the ridge on the far side of the river, he thought to look at the parole George had signed. *Return to your sovereign allegiance,* it read. *Forsake the company of fools.* Stephen tucked it back into his pocket and laughed out loud. He thought he could make it back to his ship in about five days. And he needed that time to think about how he would tell his brother.

The five days did not really help. When he was finally back in Jamestown, Stephen found various things to do before he went back to the *Susquehanna.* He spoke with the owner of the now-lost carriage and returned his horse to another planter. He stopped at an inn on the way back to the ship and bought a bowl of stew, which he stirred slowly with his spoon. He had to frame the story clearly in his mind now, and after he had done so, he finally pushed back his bench and walked miserably toward the harbor.

His brother was in his cabin, working on some papers. Stephen walked up to the door, breathed in deeply several times, and rubbed his palms on his breeches. He had to tell his brother that he had killed two members of his crew and had wounded his second-in-command, who was no doubt stirring up trouble somewhere.

When he was invited to enter, he did so, very nervously.

Captain Monroe brightened when he saw him, and rose to his feet. "Did Lady Huntington make it safely to her father?"

"She did," Stephen answered glumly.

Captain Monroe stopped, suddenly suspicious. "Why is Lieutenant Morris not here to report?"

At this, forgetting the naval protocols, Stephen sat down suddenly on a nearby chair, and the story just poured out of him. He was just talking to his brother—and, as he felt later, to his father. Captain Monroe sat down carefully and listened gravely.

"And that is what happened to all of us . . . all of it. I don't know how to say this, but if you need to have me punished, I am ready. I killed two of your men, and I don't know where Lieutenant Morris is."

Stephen stopped and held his breath. His brother had his fingers pushed together, and although he was serious, he seemed very relieved. "Stephen," he finally said, "if you had done nothing in that circumstance, *that* would have called for punishment. I am very proud of you, and I hope that any of my men would have done the same in such circumstances. But I don't know that all of them would have. You are dismissed."

The Tale of the Ribbons

TWO MONTHS LATER, IN MID-JANUARY, Captain Monroe called Stephen to his quarters. They were in port again, having been out to sea only once for a short jaunt, but to no avail. No prizes, no action, and they then had to return for supplies and water. The same day they tied up, a gentleman from town brought them a letter from General Greene in South Carolina which had been brought to him by a messenger riding a lathered horse. General Greene had just replaced General Gates after the latter's disastrous encounter with Cornwallis at Camden. The messenger from Green could not wait but had urged that the letter be delivered to Captain Monroe as soon as he arrived in port. And this, two days later, was exactly what had happened. Captain Monroe had a day to think about it, and when he summoned his brother to him, Stephen thought his brother even more serious than usual, and he was usually a serious man.

"Stephen, I am going to ask you to deliver these to General Greene's army," Captain Monroe said, handing two sealed parchments over to him. "The first is for the general. The second is for your brother."

"Robert?"

Captain Monroe smiled. "We don't have any others. Robert is still with the Maryland Line under General Morgan, and they have come south for this campaign. And the campaign here in Caroline is turning out to be far more important than anyone thought it would be—even General Washington."

"What do you mean?"

"The war is not going well up north. Clinton holds New York, and General Washington doesn't have the forces to take it, and there is nothing else he can do. So he is frustrated, and General Clinton thinks he has found the key to the war. Hold the ports and launch devastating raids from there. Now that Lord Cornwallis has Savannah and Charleston, he was supposed to just sit there. Clinton wanted a war of attrition— where we cannot get at their forces, and they refuse to meet us in main battle. Cornwallis has done some of what he was told. He has turned loose some of their fiercest fighters. Lieutenant Colonel Banastre Tarleton and Major Pembroke-Smythe are both of them—when they are on their raids—damnation in riding boots. The war here in the south has been a very dirty war, in both directions." Captain Monroe didn't say anything, but they both knew that Lieutenant Morris's attempts to hang the Tories was a good example of that.

Stephen nodded, although he didn't need to. And his brother added, "If you are going to become your enemies in the way you fight them, then why not just go over to them at once? It would save a lot of people a lot of trouble that way."

"You said that Cornwallis did *some* of what General Clinton told him."

"Yes, and it is the first good news I have heard in many months. Our Lord Cornwallis is not following his orders. Cornwallis doesn't want to hole Virginia up and starve us patriots out, but rather wants to take it by main force. So his army is on the move north. General Greene wants me to sail north and get word to General Washington and have him come south to Virginia. And if we can, to get word to the French fleet about Cornwallis's direction."

"What do you want me to do?"

"I want you to deliver this to General Greene, telling him that I have the message, and that he may consider it done. And while you are there, please greet your brother for the two of us. He is a lieutenant now, I believe, and letters from father tell me that he is one of General Morgan's most trusted aides. When your mission is done, you may return here and wait for us."

The next morning the Susquehanna set sail, and Stephen sat on his horse on the ridge above the harbor, rejoicing and bittersweet unhappy as he watched her go. He was going to see Robert, and yet his ship was sailing without him. But rather than moping about it, he pulled hard on the reins, spurred the horse, and was off down the road. His pouch was filled—with ash cake, apple leather, and hard biscuits— and he had a brace of pistols in his belt. Over his shoulder was a baldric for his sword, and he had the two letters in a secret compartment in the bottom of his pouch. If he encountered the Redcoats and they found the messages, he might swing for it, and so he resolved to fight in such a way that he would not find out if he would swing for it. It was a bright January morning, biting, but not miserable cold. He thought that, as the day advanced, he would warm up considerably. He had a week of riding before him, if the riding went well, and so he set himself to it.

Three days later he got information on the location of Greene's army from a farmwife of *decided* patriot views. Her brother and husband were both with Greene, and godspeed, she said. Two days after that, he was surprised by an advance rider for Morgan, looking for the Broad River. "It is about five miles back," Stephen said. "I just crossed it." The rider swore under his breath and wheeled to head back. "May I ride with you?" Stephen quickly asked. "I have a message for one of

Morgan's lieutenants."

"Suit yourself," the man said, and they both set off at a canter. After a few miles, Stephen saw commotion up ahead, a large body of men on the move. He stayed right next to the rider, who took them both straight to Morgan, who was meeting with some of his aides as they rode up. The rider saluted and said, "General, there is no way we can make it across the Broad before Tarleton catches up with us."

Morgan muttered to himself and then said aloud, "I don't want us fighting with our backs to water we can't ford." Pondering for a moment, he then said, "Assemble at Cowpens. Get the word to everyone to meet at Cowpens."

The aides all scattered, including the rider that had brought Stephen into the midst of the army, and General Morgan just looked at him squinting. "And who might you be?" he asked.

"My name is Stephen Monroe, brother of Robert Monroe. I have a message for him."

The general chuckled. "Any brother of Robert Monroe is a brother of mine. Can you shoot like he does?" Stephen laughed and shook his head. "More's the pity."

General Morgan wheeled in his saddle and pointed toward the rear of the column. "That's where your Marylanders are. Deliver your message and feel free to stay the night with us at Cowpens. We will need every man jack we can get. Even if you can't shoot as well as your brother, can you shoot in the right direction?"

"Aye. I can do that."

"Well, you arrived at just the right time for doing it, laddie." With that, General Morgan spurred his horse and was off to the head of the column. The word that the decision had been made to defend themselves at Cowpens had gotten around, and the column was moving off to the left now. Stephen shook his head, amazed that he had just been speaking with the great Morgan, one of the heroes of Saratoga, and then he began making his way back toward where his brother was. After just a few moments, he recognized him, still a way off, and touching the sides of his horse with his spurs, they cantered up.

"Lieutenant Monroe, I believe?" he said.

His brother jumped in the saddle and then roared, "Well, little Stephen! Well, Stephen's not so little! Stephen!" They shook hands, and Stephen handed over the letter from William. Robert looked at it curiously, and then put it inside his great coat. "Don't have time for it now," he said. "We have to find our place at what the General calls Cowpens. Such an inspiring name. From there, we will move on to an even greater victory over the Redcoats at Pig Hutch. Our names will go down in history."

Stephen laughed, remembering suddenly all the jokes that Robert used to tell at the family dinner table. And then he remembered that while William never told jokes, he always laughed the loudest at them. "Come on," Robert spoke again. "Destiny awaits."

Within half an hour, the Maryland line was settled in the place where Morgan ordered them. A long slope fell away before them, and behind them it was not that far to the summit of the hill. To their right were units from Virginia and Georgia under Triplett and Taite, and down the slope before them was a long line of South Carolina militiamen under a man named Pickens. Twilight was approaching, and Stephen could see General Morgan riding back and forth giving instructions to the troops. Out in front of Pickens' men, he had set a line of sharpshooters. The evening was cool and silent, and they could hear General Morgan's voice coming up the slope toward them.

"Look at my back!" he roared. *"That's* what the British did to me." Stephen couldn't see anything, so he looked at Robert questioningly. "Back in the French/Indian War, Morgan was flogged by the British. Some lieutenant became irritated with him and struck him with the flat of his sword. Morgan knocked him plain out with a right to the jaw. But he was court-martialed for it and given 499 lashes. Would have killed anybody else. And his back is a sight to behold. He has no love for the British."

The general's voice continued to waft up to them. "Now I want you to wait 'til Tarleton's men are fifty paces away. And then I want you to let off two shots, and only two. You Caroline boys are allus bragging you can hit a bitty squirrel at fifty paces. Well, you could fit *ten* squirrels in Tarleton's helmet. So, wait 'til they are fifty paces off, two shots, and then fall back. I don't want your line to hold. Fall back, you got that?"

After another hour of shouting his orders, cajoling, and frontier boasting for the lines below them, General Morgan finally came riding up their line. When he saw Lieutenant Monroe, he pulled up and said, "This is how we are going to take them. When our men below fall back, Tarleton is the kind of man who does not know how to retreat. And though he attacks all the time, he doesn't know how to attack. He'll come straight up the hill, and we'll fold on him." Morgan looked up and down the Maryland line. "I told those Caroline boys that you Tidewater men can shoot twice as good as they can. They allowed not, but I want you to aim for the epaulettes. Pick off the epaulettes!"

After speaking to all the men along that line, the general moved off to the Virginians. The night passed slowly. "I don't think Tarleton will attack until dawn," Robert said, "and we can sleep right here."

Then after a moment, he said, "And how did it happen that mother let you take up arms? I thought the decision had been made to wait until your eighteenth year."

"And so it was," Stephen said. "I owe my good fortune to the tale of the ribbons."

"Ribbons?" Robert said.

"Ribbons," Stephen answered. "The Redcoat colonel there in Annapolis is the most perfect coxcomb that ever walked the earth. He loves the parade grounds, and taking tea with the ladies, and walking in a stately manner around St. Anne's. Even mother thinks him insufferable, and you know how kind mother is. There was a militia to the west that would fight him if he could be bothered, but he couldn't be bothered, and I wasn't allowed to go in the militia to go fight anybody else. So one day I was inspired to decorate the horses of his small party while they were having high tea with Lady Westmore."

"A prank," Robert said. "A worthy joke, but still a joke. How did that result in you going off to the navy?"

"The Colonel's pride was offended, and he vowed that he would put me in stocks or worse."

"How did he know it was you? Surely you were not fool enough to be seen?"

"Of course not," Stephen said. "But at the sight of the pink ribbons, the Colonel went raging up and down the street, and the shopkeeper where I bought the ribbons (it turns out) was a Tory. She told him that I was the one that bought the ribbons."

"That was it?"

"Well, no. I had written a note to go with the ribbon on his horse. I didn't sign it, but once identified as the buyer of the ribbon, my sentiments were assumed to be the same as those found in the note."

"And those sentiments were . . .?"

"Mortally offensive. I had to hide for weeks until brother William came through and took me off to the navy."

"What did you say in the note?"

"It was a little poem. I don't think I should repeat it now. Mother was very embarrassed. Lady Westmore had been a friend of mother's before the war and before she married my Lord Pimples for his money and title. I didn't know that. I said I was sorry, but that didn't keep me from having to hide in the barn. Mother forgave me, but the Colonel thought it was easier to roar about in search of me than to go fight a war."

Robert bent his head over, until his chin was on his chest, and laughed quietly. As the two brothers talked, the story of what happened with their cousin George and the wounding of Lieutenant Morris and the killing of the two sailors came up. Stephen poured out the whole story, grateful for someone else to tell. "And William says I did right. But I still go over it in my mind."

"Well, I was never the reader that William was. But we see it the same way. And I always did like George. I wonder what made him not willing to thank you. But Aunt Abigail will certainly thank you, politics or no politics."

"George was angry and frightened, and he didn't want to admit that he was frightened. I hope he thinks better of it."

"But even though you did right, it is still a strange business and no mistake. In the morning, George himself might come running up this hill, and you and I, if we are minding our duty, will put a bullet into him. But if he asks for quarter, we are both bound to give it. It is like when we were children playing tag, with the same rules, only with musket balls instead of tagging. If anyone says *time,* we all have to stop. We can blow each other to bits, like good Christians, but we have to do it by the rules."

"William says this is part of living in Christendom. Lieutenant Morris says that Christendom is dead."

"Well," Robert said, looking at his long gun. "Lieutenant Morris's world seems a lot more logical to me. And a lot uglier. If I get in a fight in his world, there are no holds barred, and it might be a lot easier to win. But there is also nothing lovely or noble to fight for. So who cares if you win?" But then Robert looked sideways at Stephen. "But keep in mind that William will inherit all father's books, and for good reason. He could probably give you some better reasons."

The Battle of Cowpens

"HERE THEY COME," SAID ROBERT.

Stephen looked out over the mound of earth in front of him and squinted in the early morning light. A few cavalrymen in bright green jackets cantered out of the woods and into the meadow. They came forward to reconnoiter the ground, and see where the first line of sharpshooters were. A few puffs of smoke revealed that, and a few of the riders toppled to the ground. Some scattered shouts came up the hill.

About fifty riders then appeared in the meadow, and off on the left were kilts and scarlet jackets. "Highlanders!" Robert muttered. "Those men can fight. We shall do what we can to keep them from getting all the way up *here*." A bright row of soldiers formed up in front of the woods, green and red, scarlet and white.

"At least we can see them, " Stephen said.

"Aye," Robert answered. "One less worry. But we have others."

The first line of American sharpshooters let fly, and the smoke rose up and drifted off to the right. The British were still forming up, and about fifteen of their number were suddenly down. The sharpshooters knew how to reload quickly, and after just another moment another volley was off. Stephen could see them all running up the hill, bent halfway over, toward the second line made up of Colonel Pickens' Carolina men. Morgan was moving up and down the line, roaring, "Epaulettes and sergeants! That's all we need. Just like a turkey shoot!"

Tarleton ordered his men forward, and the way his men held their line was magnificent. They advanced steadily, and the Americans held their fire. Stephen heard Morgan going over their instructions yet again. "Two shots. Just two shots. And then fall back around to the left. Epaulettes and sergeants!"

The British got within about a hundred paces, and the order to fire was given. The roar of guns rose up from Pickens' line, and the British line wavered and halted. When they stopped, they returned fire, shouting angrily. But Morgan's men were trained to reload while moving, and the British had to stand still to reload. While they were reloading, the Carolina men hit them again. About half the British officers were down—concentrating on epaulettes was working. After the second round, the second line of Americans that day fell back. The militia moving rapidly back looked like a panic to the British cavalrymen, who did not expect much of anything else from militiamen. They spurred their horses and took out after the militiamen, who increased their speed. Some of the Americans actually broke and ran, which fortunately made the retreat look more like a rout. General Morgan was right behind Robert and Stephen now, the third line made up of Maryland and Virginia regulars.

"Fine, fine!" he yelled. "Wait till our militia boys are out of the line of fire. Hold your fire!"

As the militia streamed past them, two British field pieces opened fire on the Marylanders and Virginians. Stephen felt a thump in his chest when a cannonball struck the ground about ten yards in front of him. A moment later a shower of dirt fell out of the sky, pelting him like so many little brown hailstones. He looked over at Robert with wide eyes. Robert grinned at him. "You weren't supposed to get *dirty*," he said.

Below them the British troops formed up for a charge, preparing to come up and bayonet the remaining Americans. "Hold! Hold!" they could hear Morgan yelling. A command was given below, and Stephen, looking over the lip of earth in front of him, could see a stream of color pounding up the hill. He scooted up further and lowered the rifle that Robert had given him.

"Remember that time we went turkey hunting when you were twelve," Robert said. "We were shooting downhill then, too, and you sent more than one musket ball whistling over their bobbing little heads. Shooting downhill is tricky. Make the adjustment."

"Aye," Stephen said. "I remember."

"Hold! Hold!" Morgan was striding just behind them.

"I can do that," Stephen muttered. "But they are getting close."

"Now! *Fire!*"

The British line reeled and staggered to a stop. When they ceased their advance, Tarleton in the rear saw they were in trouble and brought his Highlanders out of reserve, sending them up the hill toward the Virginia line, off to Stephen's right. The advancing British line and the Americans gave a hot exchange for about ten minutes. Stephen had never reloaded so fast in his life before, but he could feel how slow he was compared to the men around him. Robert was getting off two shots for every shot he fired. And he was probably hitting his targets, too.

In order to meet the Highlanders' onslaught, the Virginians had to turn to face them. But when the order was given, that order was misunderstood, and they turned to march toward the rear, to some higher ground that had been marked out for them the night before. Morgan was behind the Maryland line, and the Marylanders took their cue from the Virginians and began falling back in good order.

General Morgan was grinning broadly as Stephen and Robert marched past him toward the rear. "That's not what I ordered," he said. "But it'll do sure enough. Stay steady! Steady! Come about when I say!"

The Americans had a cavalry unit that was hidden in a swale, that had come out once before in the battle. But now they emerged again because Tarleton's cavalry was pursuing the Americans up the hill. Morgan later told Robert that if the Virginians had not misunderstood their order, they would have been destroyed between the Highlanders and the British cavalry. But as the British horse were galloping up the hill, the American cavalry, under a Colonel Washington, burst out of their hiding place in the swale and charged through the British unit, wheeled around below them, and charged back through them again. While this was happening, the Virginians and Marylanders continued to march up the hill, with the British advancing steadily behind them.

Morgan was up ahead of his men, galloping across the line, looking downhill, and he kept shouting out, "Hold!" He came by Robert and Stephen and kept saying the same thing. "Lieutenant Monroe, have your men loaded and ready to wheel on my command!"

The Highlanders and the British regulars thought they had carried the day, and so they were swarming up the hill, in no good order, little more than a mob. When they were about thirty paces behind the Americans, Stephen heard General Morgan's voice rising above all the noises of battle. "Halt! Turn! *Fire!*"

The Virginians and Marylanders turned immediately, and the enemy was so close they did not even bother to raise their guns to the shoulder—they just let fly from the hip. The fire was devastating, and the British went over backwards as though they had been standing in the surf and an unexpected wave got them.

With that, the Americans charged with their bayonets, Stephen among them. Behind them, the militia that had retreated earlier under Colonel Pickens came back into the fray. After that, the British forces fell into complete disorder. Tarleton kept his head, as did his officers, but the cavalry refused to regroup, and the infantrymen fell into a panicked retreat.

Stephen had just bayoneted a soldier who had tried to discharge his rifle in Stephen's face—it had not gone off—and Stephen had some trouble getting his long rifle loose. He looked up and saw his brother in a desperate struggle with a British officer, arms locked together. The rest of the armies were streaming down the hill, but these two men were rocking back and forth, each trying to get their hands loose in order to strike the other. They came slightly toward Stephen, and Robert, whose back was toward him, stumbled over a corpse and fell backward on the ground. The British

officer fumbled for his sword, got it out, and raised it up over his head.

Stephen suddenly found his saber in his hand and leapt toward the officer with his saber pulled over his left shoulder. He swung as hard as he knew how, backhanded, and the officer's head toppled to the ground. A second later his body hit the ground beside it. Stephen stared down in stunned disbelief. That was the officer who met them outside Cornwallis' army, the man who had been so insolent to him. A moment later he realized it was the man who was going to marry Lady Huntington. Oh, my, he thought. Then he thought, *I'm glad I didn't know that when I did it.*

He turned and helped Robert to his feet. They were both shaky, for different reasons, and they looked down the slope together. The British were in a complete and total rout. "Praise Jehovah," Robert said. "Praise Jehovah."

A week earlier, Lady Huntington had made up her mind—she was not going to marry that man. It took her a day or two to realize all that this decision meant, but one of the first things she realized was that it meant that she was going to have to escape from the camp of Cornwallis. But where could she possibly go? Over to the Americans? What would *they* do with her?

There were two events that had settled it in her mind. Marriage was out of the question. Major Pembroke-Smythe was a gentleman, certainly, but he was also just like Tarleton—competent, bloodthirsty, cruel, and with no sense of humanity or remorse when it came to the war against the Americans.

The first event was one that had made her proud, and she had been surprised at why it had made her proud. Because life in the camp was extremely tedious for a lady, her father had arranged for her to spend some time with some of the local ladies, among them a Loyalist woman named Abigail Ingle, a woman with a kind and gentle face. Lady Huntington took a liking to her instantly. With just a small escort, Lady Huntington was able to call on Mrs. Ingle because her home—a very stately home—was just south of the camp, and the Americans were all to the north. There were a few other ladies there, and they all visited generally, about the weather, about the war, and some of them about their husbands. While they were talking about the war, one of the ladies, an ardent Tory, spoke about how wicked the rebels were. All of them.

Mrs. Ingle seemed provoked, but said nothing, thinking for a moment. Then she spoke, very quietly, shaking her head. "Sally, wars are terrible things, and one of the reasons they are

secrets they could go out into the hall.

Major Pembroke-Smythe was talking with Lieutenant Colonel Tarleton, and a Major Bowton was largely silent. Tarleton had just told a story that Lady Huntington could not quite make out—he had a low voice—and the men all laughed, a cold kind of laughter. Then her fiancé told a story, and his voice was not so low. As he progressed through the story, Lady Huntington felt herself grow increasingly anxious and was doing very poorly at her play. All she could do was listen to the story, with increasing horror.

She didn't get it all because the men were laughing, but she did hear, "the farmwife came out and begged us not to hurt her poor boy, who was just trying to protect the horses. But I told her that her poor boy was going to hang from the walnut tree, and if she said another word about it, his little brother would be right there next to him . . . we burned the house to the ground, of course . . . what this war needs is fewer rebels, and fewer boys growing up into rebels. Well, we did our part for the king."

Lady Huntington put her cards down on the table and folded her hands in her lap. She did not to think about it any further. She could not marry this man, and if she remained in the camp here with her father, she would have to marry him. She could not return to England. The only thing to do was to flee to the Americans. But how could she do that? What would she do then?

She did not know, and after the party had broken up she spent a great deal of time in her chambers thinking about what she could do. She had no idea, but one thing comforted her. She was doing the same thing that Stephen had done. He had seen a great wickedness on his own side, and he did what was most necessary to do. She had seen that these men surrounding Cornwallis were just as wicked, and she had to do what was necessary.

Over the next few days, she took a greater interest in the talk about the war that was constant, both at dinner and after. Earlier she had just paid attention to who was winning and who losing, but now she began paying attention to names of places, and where armies were, and where they were thought to be going. That was how she learned that the American army under General Greene had departed from Charlotte and was marching southeast. Morgan had been sent to the southwest, and Tarleton and Smythe were to be sent out after him. If they could take out Morgan, then Cornwallis would have a clear march all the way up into Virginia. That is not what General Clinton had told him to do, but that was the way that Lord Cornwallis thought to bring glory to himself.

"There is going to be fighting north of here then," thought Lady Huntington. "I will have to make my way to the northeast and, if I can find him, ask General Greene if *he* knows what to do with me."

She knew that there were almost no guards on the south side of the encampment, down toward the Ingle home, and so the same morning that Tarleton's forces were about to depart to the north, she arose at two in the morning and walked steadily south. She thought she could make it to the Ingle house by dawn, and she thought also that if she begged Abby Ingle, that the kind lady would give her a carriage.

And that is what she did—a carriage, provisions, a servant driver, and indeed, she showed the greatest kindness of all: she asked no questions. "I will write you when I may," Lady Huntington said. "But I am forever in your debt."

The carriage disappeared south down the road, and as Mrs. Ingle turned back into the house, she smiled to herself. *I wouldn't marry him either.*

Pursuit up the Chesapeake

CAPTAIN MONROE STOOD NEAR THE BOW OF the *Susquehanna* and looked anxiously northwards. The winds were contrary, and he was not making the headway that he needed. They were now near the mouth of the Chesapeake Bay, but he wanted to make it as far up the bay as they could before he sent a messenger overland to General Washington.

He was concentrating so intently on the problem of time that he did not at first hear the lookout above him. "Sail ahoy!" There was a scuffling on the deck behind him as the sailors clambered to their assigned stations. After a moment, his mate appeared at his right shoulder. "Sail ahoy, Cap'n. Abaft the beam. Starboard side." Captain Monroe shook his head to clear it, somewhat annoyed with himself and then strode quickly toward the stern. When he was amidships, he pulled out his spyglass and put it to his eye.

After a moment of hard looking, he pulled the glass down again. "Can't make out her flag," he muttered. "But she is closing fast, and she has guns."

He thought for a moment and then shouted to the helmsman. "Left full rudder! Come about hard!" He then looked at his mate and nodded. The mate knew what his men aloft had to do with the sails to keep the *Susquehanna* coming about in a complete circle, and he was instantly up in the rigging, barking orders. The ship turned nicely and came about in nearly a perfect circle.

On the other ship William Morris looked on with admiration. "Nicely done," he said to himself. His new ship was a privateer, the *Constant,* and he had decided that if the Continental Congress was not going to recognize his abilities and achievements, then he would have to take matters into his own hands and make his own glory—the kind of glory that could not be shuffled off to the side for grubby partisan reasons. After his scrape with Stephen over the hanging of the Tories, he had made his way north to Philadelphia and contacted some old friends who had money to outfit a ship and papers to make the privateering legal enough. With that, he was able to raise a crew of competent sailors, but who, when it came to their catechism, were generally worthless fellows. They were men who did not scruple about who they might fight, or what they might do, so long as the rum was good and the wind was at their backs. They had already had good success with two British merchants, and Captain Morris, as he now styled himself, was doing well with his plan to make himself indispensable to the colonial effort. That way, if Stephen Monroe ever decided to press the point of their conflict, or if his brother tried to make anything of his failure to come back to the *Susquehanna,* then he would be in a position to appeal to his contributions to the war. *If it is politics they want, it is politics they will get.*

But now, here, was the *Susquehanna,* alone. Captain Morris knew his old ship well. The *Constant* was four guns to the advantage and was lighter in the keel. She handled better, and Morris thought he had a clear hand. He knew that his crew would not balk at showing no quarter. A little pirate work, no mercy, send them all to Davy Jones, and that would be it. All he had to do was settle who was the rightful captain of the *Susquehanna* by sending the *Susquehanna* to the bottom. The new order of the ages would certainly allow him to settle a personal matter, and he knew the cut of his crew well enough to know that they would enjoy the fight and enjoy the plunder still more. But there was no sense in pretending.

"Boys!" he called out, at the top of his voice. "Boys, this is my old ship, captained by the man who stole my rightful place. I have a score to settle with him, and I pray that you'll indulge me. If you do, I will return it to you with compliments and with a handsome profit. Aye?" With that, all the crew within earshot roared *aye* back at him, and he knew that those who were not within earshot would get the word. They would not be troubled by anything like a flag. What was a common flag between enemies?

The *Susquehanna* had at first swung away from them, but then had come back around. They were now sailing straight toward one another and were due to pass one another's port sides. Captain Monroe still had his glass to his eye, trying to make out their flag. For his part, Captain Morris knew that Captain Monroe would be looking closely, and so he stepped behind a cabin. The gun ports of both ships were fully opened, and the crews of both ships were at their battle stations. But at that moment the flag on the *Constant* unfurled clearly, and Captain Monroe put down his eyeglass with relief. He turned to his mate and said, "Americans." Word traveled fast, and the crew of the *Susquehanna* all stood back in relief, relaxing.

Turning back to the gunwale, Captain Monroe leaned on the rail and prepared to shout out greetings as they passed. As their bows came even with each other, the ships were very close—only about fifty yards apart. Captain Monroe waited for a moment and then cupped his hands to shout out a greeting. Just then a figure, oddly familiar, stepped out onto the deck of the other ship, and Captain Monroe stopped and pulled his glass back up again. Morris!

Just at that moment a roar came from the other ship, and billows of smoke blew out from her port side. A second later, the port side of the *Susquehanna* erupted in an explosion of splinters and fragments of wood. The crew of the *Susquehanna* was entirely unprepared for the broadside, and for a number of seconds none of the survivors did anything. Then Captain Monroe recovered from his shock and surprise and roared out, "Right full rudder! Hard about, hard about!" He needed to get away for a space, assess the damages, and evaluate the wind. As the *Susquehanna* pulled away, the *Constant* was coming about to port in order to follow them hard.

The chief gunner bolted up from below. "We are badly hurt on the port side, Cap'n. Half our guns are out. We need to fight on the starboard side, as much as can be. Sorry, Cap'n." Captain Monroe nodded and looked up at the sails. This would take everything he had, and he wasn't sure he had it. *Morris.* What was *he* doing here?

The battle lasted for three hours, although it would be more accurate to say that it was three hours of sailing and maneuvering, with brief interludes of violent combat. Captain Monroe managed to have almost all the *Susquehanna's* broadsides delivered from starboard, and for his part, Captain Morris began to get frustrated at his inability to get Monroe into a position he knew Monroe did not want to be in. The damage to the *Susquehanna's* portside battery was obvious from the *Constant,* and so the reason for the Susquehanna's complex maneuvers was also obvious. What was equally clear was that Captain Morris couldn't

stop it from happening. By the third hour of their contest of seamanship, punctuated with violent blasts from the cannons, Morris was pacing the deck, swearing indiscriminately. Suddenly a sailor appeared from below decks. "We're taking on water bad, Cap'n. We need some more men for the pumps."

Morris glared at him and then swore again. "Take them from the gun crews." Then he turned and ordered the crew manning the sails to throw up every piece of canvas they had. And with that for an ignominious end to their attempted treachery, the *Constant* simply veered north and headed up the bay. The *Susquehanna* was the heavier ship of the two and would not be able to catch up with the *Constant* under any conditions. But in addition, she had also taken on some water and was listing to port.

On the *Susquehanna* Captain Monroe smiled grimly to himself. They didn't really need to be fast—there was no way out of the bay at the north end—and so the *Susquehanna* could just follow at their leisure. But Morris must have some place in the Chesapeake where he *thought* he could go.

Lady Huntington sat quietly in the drawing room of General Greene's headquarters. In the next room, there was murmuring, some quiet male voices were discussing (as she supposed) what to do with her. She had arrived at the outskirts of the American camp unannounced, released the servant with the carriage to return to the Ingles, and then walked up to an astonished sentry guarding a crossroads outside the camp. He had sent his companion into the camp to get an escort for her, and then he spent the time he had with this very beautiful lady scratching his head, trying to think of something to say. After an agonizing half hour, two soldiers appeared to take her to the General. They had done so with dispatch, and she had a brief interview with the General—who appeared to be a very kindly man—and had been sitting out here in the drawing room ever since. There was an adjutant there to attend to her if she needed something, but for all that, she just sat quietly, hands folded on her lap.

It was late afternoon now, and suddenly her head turned to hear a commotion on the front porch of the house. The door flew open, and Stephen Monroe stepped in. He looked at the adjutant who was standing behind his small desk in the entryway and said, "I have an urgent message for General Greene." The adjutant nodded and stepped quickly toward the door where the General was.

"Stephen!" Lady Huntington said.

Startled, Stephen swiveled around. "Lady Huntington!" He stopped with shock for a moment and then took two steps toward her. But by that time the General and his aides came hurriedly out of the back room. Normally, a general would never come out to meet a messenger, but General Greene knew that Morgan was being pursued by Tarleton and was very anxious for any news. Stephen hesitated and then turned back toward the General. The General was looking at him quizzically, eyebrows up.

"General Greene, I have wonderful news. Morgan has routed Tarleton at Cowpens. It was a total victory for our forces, with very few of Tarleton's men left to tell about it."

Several of the General's aides shouted, but the General himself just puffed out his cheeks and said, "*Well.*" Then he rubbed his chin. "Well," he said again.

In the general commotion that followed over the next few minutes, it became apparent to the others there that Lady Huntington and Stephen knew one another. "And how is that?" asked the General.

Stephen turned a little red, although he was not sure why, and said, "Lady Huntington was first taken captive by our ship at sea. When we came to port, we had her escorted to the camp of Lord Cornwallis, where her father and, um, former fiancé, were serving in the British army."

It was Lady Huntington's turn to blush, and she said, "I suppose he is still my fiancé. I never spoke to him about my intent to leave. But I could not speak to him."

"I am sorry to have to be the one to inform you of this, my

lady, but Major Smythe was killed at the battle of Cowpens," Stephen said.

Lady Huntington flushed again. "Are you certain of this?" she cried. She was greatly relieved. Stephen was not sure how much to say about it, and decided he should give the details later, when there were not so many observers of their conversation. "I saw it with my own eyes, ma'am."

The General was following everything with interest. "Major Smythe was your fiancé, then?"

"Yes, General, he was. The marriage was arranged for me while I was still in England, but when I determined for myself what kind of man he was, I decided that marriage to him was not possible for me. But I could not decline the match and remain where I was, so I came over to you. And again, I am sorry to place such an imposition upon you."

"Not at all," the General started to say, but Stephen saw that he really was discommoded about what to do.

"General, may I make a suggestion?" Stephen said.

"Certainly," the General said.

"I am a midshipman on the Susquehanna, the ship commanded by my brother, Captain Monroe. When you sent word to have our ship go north to get word to General Washington about Cornwallis heading toward Virginia . . . oh, what a ninnyhammer!" With that, Stephen flipped open the pouch hanging by his side and pulled out the letter that Captain Monroe had written to the General and handed it over to him. "That is how I came to be with General Morgan at Cowpens. I was delivering a letter there, and this one is for you. I just happened to encounter Morgan's men first, and I got caught up in the excitement when Tarleton's men caught up with us."

The General opened the letter and read it deliberately. When he was done, he nodded his head and then looked back at Stephen. "You said you had a suggestion."

"Oh, yes sir." Stephen said. "My parents live in Annapolis, and they would be happy to show hospitality to Lady Huntington until they made some introductions and arrangements for her. I could escort her there and afterwards try to meet my brother's ship, which has sailed up the bay. In any case, I have nothing else to do until I find my ship or my ship finds me."

The General looked across at two of his colonels. They both nodded, glad for a simple solution, at least as far as they were concerned. They did not want Lady Huntington in their camp when angry emissaries began arriving from Lord Cornwallis. The rules of war did not really give guidance for such things, and it would be far easier to just say that the lady was not there.

"Stephen," Lady Huntington asked, "are you sure your parents would . . . not mind?"

"I am certain."

The next morning a carriage pulled away from General

Greene's camp, driven by an elderly servant. Stephen and Lady Huntington sat in the back and had many hours to converse about all that had happened since they had parted some weeks before.

Lady Huntington told Stephen that she had heard about what he did for his cousin George. "How did you hear of *that?*" Stephen cried.

"From George's mother. The Ingle home is just on the other side of Cornwallis's camp. George may not have shown his gratitude, but his mother was as grateful as any woman I have ever seen. She said that she was going to write to your mother and express her gratitude fully. When we get to your home, you will no doubt get to see her letter."

Stephen looked out the side of the carriage. "I still think about what I did," he said. "But my conscience doesn't bother me. I know it would if I had acted the other way."

"I was very proud of you, Stephen, when I first heard. And it was what you did that gave me courage to leave. I overheard Major Smythe boasting of doing something very much like what Morris was going to do."

After a short silence, Stephen said, "There is something else I have to tell you. I don't want you to hear it from anyone else, although I don't really want you to hear it from anyone really."

"What is that?" she said.

"The reason I saw Major Smythe killed at Cowpens is that I was the one who did it. He was about to kill my brother,

Robert, but I got to him first. Please don't think I am bragging
... I am not ... I didn't want to tell you, but I am sure you will
hear from someone."

"I didn't think you were bragging. How . . . how did it
happen?"

"It was a terrible thing. I cut his head off. With my saber."

They both sat quietly, content with the silence. Finally,
Lady Huntington said, "Well, Stephen, all I can say is that
you have become an upright man. You went off to war
because you were an impudent boy playing tricks with
ribbons. And you have done some hard things, but these are
the sorts of things that men must do."

"Who told you about the ribbons?"

"Your brother, the captain. He told me about your famous
ribbons at the ball we went to."

"The *ball!* You must tell me about what happened there.
William would say nothing whatever about it."

The Fight at Two Williams

CAPTAIN MONROE HAD GUESSED WHICH PORT along the western shore of the Chesapeake was the closest to General Washington's army and had dropped a messenger off there with a sealed letter for the general. They had then sailed north along the east side of the bay, and now they were on the west side, headed south again. The lookouts had instructions to look for anything suspicious and to report anything that looked as though it might be related in any way to the *Constant*. They were working their way back down the bay, aware that if they had passed the *Constant*, their adversary could already have put out to sea, headed south, and been far away by this point. But Captain Monroe remembered that there was no need for the *Constant* to break off hostilities by heading up into the bay—they could just as easily have gone in any of the other directions with a lot of open sea before them. And so he thought that they must have some hiding place to tie up in or a place with many friends.

When they got near the South River, the Captain was seized with a suspicion and sent a skiff up the river to see what was there. He remembered Morris saying something once about that river in a way that bespoke real familiarity. The skiff was gone half the morning while *Susquehanna* rolled patiently at anchor out past the mouth of the river. When the skiff returned, two burley sailors—they had been chosen for their prowess at rowing—clambered back on board. "Aye, Cap'n," one of them said. "She's there alright, tied up in the bright sunshine."

Captain Monroe walked over to the gunwale and stood, looking out over the water. He was rubbing his hand along his jaw thoughtfully, trying to decide what he should do. While he was there, his first mate came up to him and stood silently by. He had earned the Captain's trust in a number of different encounters, and he knew that if his counsel was wanted, he needn't press to give it. And so he just stood there quietly.

"The problem, Timothy, is this," the Captain said. "These are Americans. They attacked us on the open sea, and had we sunk them, or they us, the thing would have been over. But here they are, in a friendly port, and they have apparently been attacking British merchant ships. They are Americans, and while Morris is absent from his post on our ship, that is the kind of thing that could be dragged into endless disputes, or into courts, or even before Congress. Or we could sail to Annapolis, and report what they did to the governor. But they would simply deny it, and we would have words, more words, and then more words after that. But I, for my part, do not care to just sail off and leave them with their treachery unchallenged."

The Captain then turned, and looked straight at Timothy. "What say you?" the Captain said.

"My counsel is this, if you must have it," Timothy said. "In the midst of this war, we don't have courts that can deal with this. But we do have a custom that can do it."

"What do you mean?"

"I mean that we should sail up river, and tie up near the *Constant,* and that you should approach their ship, and ask for an audience with Lieutenant Morris. He probably styles himself Captain now, but not for my money. If he gives it, then you should recount for him the fact that he attacked you without provocation and with little success. If he hopes for greater success in the future, he might try his hand at it again in the morning. You will be outside town, armed, and waiting on his convenience."

"You mean a *duel?*" Captain Monroe spoke with real contempt in his voice.

"Aye, Cap'n, after a manner of speaking."

"I hate dueling," Captain Monroe said. "Roosters strutting and roosters fighting."

"Aye, Cap'n, but hear me out. This would not be a duel because some fine lady batted her eyelashes at the wrong gentleman. It would not be over some slight to your personal honor made by a gentleman without honor. This is not a duel that way—it would just be the continuation of our battle. But the practice of dueling is common enough that the courts would allow for you to continue your battle with Morris . . . even though he is an American.

"I will think about it."

"Aye, aye. And Cap'n, one more thing. Doesn't the Good Book have generals fighting instead of their armies? That ain't dueling, not the kind you hate."

Two hours later, the *Susquehanna* was coming up river, and came suddenly around the last bend before the docks. Some of the sailors on the *Constant* saw her, and one of them dashed off to the captain's quarters to give the word. Captain Morris appeared topside almost immediately and watched closely as the *Susquehanna* maneuvered to dock. There was no sign of any warlike demeanor. After she tied off, nothing happened for a few moments, and then a gangplank went down. A solitary figure in dress uniform came down the plank and walked purposefully toward the *Constant.*

Captain Monroe was piped aboard and was saluted by the men on deck. Captain Morris was standing there to greet him, and the two men saluted one another. "I would ask for a private audience with you below decks . . . in your

stepped back, eying each other to make sure the other was unarmed, and when they had done so, they both turned to watch the combatants.

Both men lifted their swords as experienced fighters do and circled one another carefully. Captain Monroe was the first to move, and he stepped lightly toward Morris, and the swords clashed briefly. The sound of it echoed off through the trees. They tested one another this way for a few moments, watching for reflexes and measuring the stance and pace of the other. Once they had both warmed to their work, the pace picked up a little, and the sharp sounds of metal on metal filled the meadow.

They were each fighting with a seaman's saber and not with rapiers or the old-fashioned broadswords. This meant that they were in closer to each other than they otherwise would have been, and they each had to move much more quickly to counter each cut and thrust. Timothy was amazed at the swordsmanship and stood transfixed.

After they had been sparring this way for about ten minutes, they fell apart, both breathing heavily. A moment later, they went back to it, and Timothy was expecting them to be increasingly tired as the time went on. But from the very start of the second round, both men exploded, and it was hard for either of the seconds to see what was happening at all—and they were standing quietly off to the side, with nothing to do but concentrate on *trying* to see. How was it

possible for these men, each one fighting in a frenzy, to have any idea of where the next blow was coming from, and to have a sword there to counter it? But that is what they were doing, several times a second.

Captain Morris stepped back three paces suddenly, and Captain Monroe was right after him. He was raining blows down on Captain Morris, almost as though he were chopping wood with his saber, and Morris kept fending them off and stepped back again. Suddenly some wet leaves under Captain Morris's left foot slipped away from him, and he went down hard. Captain Monroe stepped forward, caught himself, and then stood back deliberately, straightening up as he did so. Captain Monroe touched his forehead with his saber.

Captain Morris sprang to his feet, angry and irritated. "You and your damn Christendom!" he shouted and lunged at Captain Monroe. But his anger made him careless, and Captain Monroe knocked Morris's saber into the dirt with a downward slash and then came back again with a strong thrust to his opponent's midsection. Morris gasped, staggered, and went down on one knee. And then, dropping his sword, he carefully put his hands to the ground, laid himself down, and died.

Captain Monroe stood back and looked at Captain Morris's second. "Was it a just fight?" he said. "Aye, it was just," the man replied. After Captain Monroe had rested himself for a time, he and Timothy helped Captain Morris's second place the body over his saddle. The two men then mounted and headed back from the promontory down to the harbor where the *Susquehanna* was moored.

They rode in silence for about half an hour. Timothy broke the silence when they were almost to the edge of town. "Cap'n, if you can spare a minute, I need to run into the Crown and Coin for just a moment."

Captain Monroe looked sideways at him. "Bit early for a drink, even for a mate."

"Oh, not for a drink, Cap'n. I have to tell a friend something." Timothy had been friends with the tavern keeper there for many years, and the night before he had gone to visit him after the interview between Monroe and Morris.

Captain Monroe nodded and stayed mounted on his horse outside the tavern while Timothy dashed inside. True to his word, he was there for just several moments. When he was back in the saddle, they turned their horses toward the south of town, right next the harbor. They had to return their horses to the stable, and they could walk to the ship from there.

"What did you have to tell your friend?"

Timothy looked sheepish. "It wasn't so much conversation, if you take my meaning. There were some sailors from the *Constant* in there last night, and they were all talking pretty loud about the duel ... about the fight this morning. So I placed a bet on the whole thing, just to steady them a bit."

"You bet on the fight?"

Timothy feigned a hurt look. "I could see a problem, Cap'n, if I had bet *against* you. But the main reason I did it was to keep those drunks from bellowing on all night about it."

They rode on for a minute, and then Timothy added, "And there is one other thing. I told my friend that if the promontory didn't have a name, I had one for him. And if it already had a name, they should change it. He said folks just called it the cliffs. So I told him what they should name it. And if a tavern owner can't name a place like that, I don't know who can."

"And what did you suggest?"

"Well, first I thought of Two Captains, you and Morris both being captains like, but I thought that wasn't good because he wasn't really a captain. But you both had Christian names of William, and *that* was honest as paint, and so I told him to make sure the promontory would get the name of Two Williams. He said he would do it, too."

Captain Monroe just smiled and shook his head, but Timothy thought he was pleased. After they had returned the horses, they walked back toward the ship and then up the gangplank. Captain Monroe then turned to Timothy and said, 'Prepare to cast off. North to Annapolis."

"Aye, aye, sir," Timothy said.

Meeting in Annapolis

WHY DO YOU WANT TO KNOW ABOUT THE BALL? Lady Huntington asked.

"Because my brother came back from it a perfect storm cloud and would not speak of it for anything," Stephen replied. "I cannot imagine what happened."

Lady Huntington laughed. "I am not sure I would have spoken of it easily either. At least not right away."

"But what was it? You said that he told you the ribbon story at the ball. But why would that . . .?"

"No," Lady Huntington said, "that was just small conversation on the way there. I confess I did not know what to make of it, and I believe your brother thought that I was being haughty. We were both discomfited to a great degree. And I just did not know what to make of a young American who became a midshipman for his brother because he tied some ribbons in some horse tails. I did not say much, but I don't believe I was unpleasant. But by the time we got to the ball, we were both most uncomfortable."

"So what was it?" Stephen asked.

"It appears silly to me now. But there was another officer there who thought himself quite gallant. He asked me to dance several times, and your brother was not at all pleased. I have to confess that I was not that pleased either—the young man's gallantry was not matched by any particular knowledge of the dance. I don't think your brother was unhappy with me, but he most certainly was unhappy with that young man"

Stephen didn't say anything, but just continued to look expectantly.

"Well, in between dances, your brother came to me—quite formally—and asked if I was in need of someone to speak to the young officer. I was perhaps annoyed that your brother felt responsible for my social engagements when his office was simply that of my captor. He was just being thoughtful, but a little bit jealous too. I saw the jealousy and said that my situation was quite accommodate, and I thanked him. He bowed stiffly, and only asked me to dance once through the rest of the evening, then escorted me back to the ship that evening without a word. That's all."

"That's it? He offered to chase off a horse fly that was annoying a lady, and the lady would rather annoy him than let him do it?

Lady Huntington smiled and lifted one eyebrow. "You make very free, Midshipman Monroe."

Stephen laughed and sat back in his seat. He said nothing more, but he understood now. And he thought with great satisfaction about the moment when he would announce to his brother that Lady Huntington was staying with their parents. It would almost be as much fun as the ribbons.

"Your brother is a very taciturn man," Lady Huntington said.

"Only in certain places," Stephen replied. "But in battle, he speaks readily and loudly enough. And when the family is seated at table together, and my brother Robert is telling his stories, William laughs the loudest and the longest. He is only quiet . . ."

"Quiet when?" Lady Huntington asked.

"When there is a lady present. And then he is very quiet. I am astonished he spoke to you as much as he did."

On the last day before they arrived in Annapolis, Lady Huntington asked Stephen if he would tell her what he had learned since he had left home. "I don't know your parents, and maybe something like that will help me talk with them. What did they think of you leaving? And how will they notice you have changed? And are you sure . . .?"

"Yes, I am sure. My parents have told me the story, which I shall apparently have to tell you, about how my father showed up at our family home with my mother, fresh off the boat from Scotland. Everyone took it well, especially my mother. She will make you feel most welcome."

"But she . . . and your father . . . weren't they . . . ?"

"No, not at the time. It had nothing to do with the hospitality. And my mother has always been the most hospitable of women. Except for the time I had to spend in the barn, and that wasn't her fault." Stephen did not add what he already suspected about his brother, for fear that the lady would quite refuse to go to the Monroe home.

"So Stephen, I fear you have changed the subject. In what ways will your mother say you have changed."

"I did change the subject, but inadvertently. I am happy to tell you. We are going to see my parents, and as I have been thinking quite a bit about talking with them, I have also been thinking about all the things they warned me about. They were things that I just did not believe they understood. I had read Mr. Paine's book many times . . . have you heard of Mr. Paine?"

"Oh, quite," said Lady Huntington.

"My parents seemed to me to be far more concerned with what his infidel opinions would do to me than they were concerned with what the British might do to me. And I did not know why my parents would not see the world as clearly as he did. I confess that I was entirely bigoted against the English and could not believe that anyone good could have any loyalty to the king."

"But surely . . ." Lady Huntington started to say.

"I know," Stephen said, "but every time someone would try to explain it to me, I just thought they were temporizing and were not as patriotic as I. But my brother is a great captain at sea, and I could not dispute his patriotism—or his goodness. And though Lieutenant Morris unsettled me, I could see that he was a very great patriot, and not a good man. I fear that I was just like my cousin George. When I went off to war, terribly excited, I would not see any good in my foe or any evil among our own patriots. George did just exactly the same thing."

"If life were easy to understand, then war would just make it easier. But the affairs of nations are difficult in the best of times, and when men go to war things can get just that much more confused."

Stephen looked up to the front of the carriage—the servant had pulled off to the far right side of the road. Up ahead he could see a column of troops coming. "Lobsterbacks!" he exclaimed.

"Lobsterbacks?" Lady Huntington said.

"Excuse me, Redcoats . . . that is . . . British troops." It suddenly dawned on Stephen that they might have to have a story prepared. Who was she? Who was he? What were they doing? Where were they going? He was on the lip of his seat peering up ahead. The troops were foot soldiers, marching doggedly south toward them in two columns. No sign of any officers. The soldiers would probably march on by. But suppose they didn't . . .

"I cannot believe I didn't think of needing to be prepared with a story," Stephen muttered.

"Well, tell as much of the truth as may be," Lady Huntington said. "It is easier to remember that way." Stephen was rolling over various possibilities in his mind and didn't like any of them. But when the head of the column reached them, the soldiers appeared absolutely uninterested in them and just marched steadily forward. Stephen silently blew out a little breath of relief without looking like that was what he was doing, and that was the moment he saw the mounted soldiers, bringing up the rear of the column. There must have been several hundred foot soldiers, and after them, cavalry. Stephen could see the plumes of the officers. As they got closer, Stephen suddenly rammed himself to the back of his carriage seat.

"Lady Huntington!"

She looked at him, startled.

"It's the Colonel! The one from Annapolis! Colonel Ribbons!"

"What's his name?"

"Colonel Stibbons. I kind of wrote a poem about him. . . . I didn't tell you that part."

Lady Huntington looked worried. "Does he know you?"

"I don't know. I'm not sure. He knows my name, for certain. And he has probably seen me around Annapolis.

But I don't know if he put my name and face together. What are they all doing? Maybe they are marching south to meet up with Cornwallis ..."

As they approached the mounted officers, Stephen prayed desperately for them to be able to ride on by. But he had forgotten the great interest in conversation that Colonel Stibbons would always display whenever there was a lady present, and he had a beautiful lady present with him.

And to be sure, the Colonel gave a command when they were within hailing distance, and the horses came slowly to a stop. The foot soldiers continued to march along—it would not be difficult to catch up with them. The Colonel touched his helmet gallantly, bowed slightly to Lady Huntington, and greeted Stephen.

"Good afternoon, sir," the Colonel said.

Stephen quietly gave another prayer, this one of thanksgiving. The Colonel did not recognize him. "Good afternoon, Colonel," Stephen said. "May I introduce Miss Watson? My name is Stephen, Stephen Fletcher."

"My name is Colonel Stibbons," the Colonel said. "And I am most pleased and gratified to make your acquaintance. Where you are going?"

Stephen remembered Lady Huntington's advice. "We are traveling to visit some distant family in Annapolis. We came most recently from the Ingle plantation in Virginia. Miss Watson is my cousin, and I came up from North Carolina to meet her there and escort her to the Watsons of Annapolis. Perhaps you are acquainted?"

The Colonel *was* acquainted with them—they were the most prominent Loyalist family in the Annapolis area. Stephen knew that the Colonel had been at more than one ball at the Watsons, and inventing a connection (but distant enough that he was unlikely to be able to contradict anything) was the best way to signal that the two of them were nothing but good Tory travelers.

They visited for ten minutes more, in which the Colonel flirted shamelessly with Lady Huntington, to little effect. He aroused a smile or two, but this was only because Lady Huntington was laboring hard to give no offense, while at the same time giving no encouragement to him to remember her at all. She needn't have worried—the Colonel was the kind of man who would strut and boast whenever a lady was present, but he actually paid very little attention to them. He thought of them as something of a feminine mirror, in which he could simply admire himself. *That* had gone into Stephen's poem also.

When the conversation was finally over, the Colonel begged them to give their regards to the Watsons and hoped ardently that providence would allow their paths to cross at some future date. As the carriage pulled away from the rear of the cavalry, Lady Huntington twisted around to watch the departing column. When they were well away, she turned back around. "Lobsterback!" she said.

Late the following day, Captain Monroe walked slowly up Prince George Street and made his way toward the family home. He had gotten word that the British forces in Annapolis had departed south, and this meant he could come into the harbor of Annapolis directly. This he had done and waited until the ship was tied up, the sailors given their time to return from liberty, and a remaining watch set to remain on the *Susquehanna*.

He was pleased and gratified to be able to visit his parents. They would be able to remain in Annapolis long enough to resupply the ship and to make the significant repairs that the battle with the *Constant* had required. Unless they had to put to sea for some emergency, they would be here for three weeks at least.

Captain Monroe was longer getting home than he had anticipated—he kept meeting old friends and acquaintances who wanted to speak with him for a moment. When he finally came up to the house, he closed the white wooden gate behind him, turned back toward the house, and was astonished to see Stephen standing on the front porch, grinning at him. "Stephen!" he exclaimed. "I thought . . ." he trailed off.

"I am here on orders from General Gates," Stephen said. "So you needn't worry about *that*." William approached the porch, came up the stairs two at a time, shook Stephen's hand, and then embraced him. "What . . . how?" he began.

"Oh, we will tell stories well into the night," Stephen said. "But in case you haven't heard the good news, Morgan took Tarleton at Cowpens. I was there, and so was Robert. He is in good health and sends his regards. And Cornwallis is coming north into Virginia."

"Thank God he is moving. Perhaps we can do something," William said.

"But come inside, our parents are waiting." Stephen was just grinning at him, and William was not sure what it could signify. As he stepped across the threshold, he heard his mother's voice in the kitchen, and just a second later Jenny Monroe burst through the kitchen door, followed by two servants and another woman. William picked his mother up and spun around with her. His father came out of the library on the south side of the house, beaming, and shook his hand heartily. When the initial greetings were over, William looked around at the house again, glad to be back, and it was then that he saw Lady Huntington. The surprise was far, far, beyond Stephen's expectations. It was almost as though he had taken a blow in the face. He actually took a step backward, recovered himself, and then bowed stiffly. Everyone else laughed happily.

When he had regained his composure, William himself smiled, but then said, "It is clear that everyone here has me at a marked disadvantage. Not that I need to know, but is there an explanation?"

And, of course, there was . . . the whole chain of events, from Stephen's confrontation of Lieutenant Morris, to the word that Lady Huntington received of Stephen's courage from his Tory aunt, and how it gave her courage to flee her marriage to a foul man. After dinner, Stephen told the entire story of Cowpens, and William was able to tell the story of his fight with William Morris.

"A duel?" his mother said.

Everyone laughed again, because William had been at great pains to explain how it was not a duel. When the laughter had died down, William spoke again.

"There is one thing we must still address. Lady Huntington, I am afraid that you are to live among patriots now, and even if that were not enough, I am sure the actions you have taken will cause your family to disown you and remove your title. We will have to come to know you by your Christian name."

Lady Huntington smiled. "Yes, that had occurred to me. From this time on, I am no longer Lady Huntington . . . though it is an ancient and honored family name, and I am sorry to have to part with it. My name is Elise. Elise . . ." and here she looked at Stephen and smiled again . . . "Elise Watson."

Late that night, after long conversation, Stephen made his way up to his old bedchamber. The candle he was holding was just a stub and kept threatening to go out. He set it down on the nightstand next to his bed, noticed a bit of paper there, and looked at it more closely. It was a letter that his parents, in all the catching up and telling of stories, had forgotten to tell him about. Stephen turned it over, and his eyes widened when he saw that it was from his cousin, George Ingle. Stephen quickly opened the seal, and holding the candle over it, read it smiling.

Glossary

ABAFT THE BEAM alongside the middle of the ship
ACCOMMODATE suitable
ADJUTANT a military assistant
AFTER RAIL the rail at the stern of the ship
AMIDSHIPS the middle of the ship
BASTION a fortress
BOW the front of the ship
CHURLISH acting sullen
COXCOMB a dandy, someone who is vain about his appearance
CUSSEDNESS ornery
DISCOMMODED made uncomfortable
EFFETE to be a dandy or effeminate
ENSIGN a naval flag which sailors salute when boarding
EPAULETTES insignia on the shoulders, marking an officer
GO TO DAVY JONES to sink to the bottom of the sea
IGNOMINIOUS disgraceful
IMPERIOUS bossy
IMPRESS to draft or require involuntary service from
IN A TRICE in a mere moment
LATHERED condition a horse gets in after running hard
LOYALIST a Tory, an American loyal to the crown
PORT the left side of the ship
PRIVATEER a private ship authorized to fight as a man of war
PROMONTORY a cliff or bluff
RECONNOITER to go scout something out
SOPHISTS relativists who don't believe in objective truth
SORTIE a small military excursion
STARBOARD the right side of the ship
STERN the back of the ship
TACITURN quiet, silent
TORY an American loyalist, one who remained loyal to the crown
WHIG an American patriot, one who supported the resistance
    to King George